The Voice in Hidden Creek

EDDIE HARDEN

PipStones Publishing
P.O. Box 4507
Fort Walton Beach, Florida 32549
www.pipstones.com

Author, Eddie Harden
Editors: Abigail Turner, Deborah Hoffman & Elizabeth Omoh
Cover Illustrator: Robert Sauber

Library of Congress Control Number: 2025918919
Copyright ©2025; Published in 2025

ISBN-13: 979-8-9889427-7-1, Hardback
ISBN-13: 979-8-9889427-8-8, Paperback
ISBN-13: 979-8-9889427-9-5, Ebook

For Worldwide Distribution.
Printed in The United States of America.

Dedication

*I want to dedicate this book to the Lord Jesus Christ who gave
me life, and saved it when I was twenty-five.*

*I also want to dedicate this to my wife, Rhonda, of 47 years.
She is the finest woman I have ever known.*

*Together, they have inspired and encouraged
me every step of the way.*

*And finally, I offer a blessing to each reader
who absorbs the message of this book:*

*The voice of the Lord can change your life,
and the lives of others, if you choose to listen.*

Contents

Introduction

How would you like to hear the voice of God and have it change everything in your life? Sometimes you don't understand why in the moment, but later you see His hand clearly at work.

That is the purpose of *The Voice in Hidden Creek.* This story shows how obedience to God—even when it doesn't make sense—can lead to wonders only He can bring. It follows a Tennessee high school principal and a janitor whose decisions to listen to the Lord fulfill a promise that had been hidden for decades.

After more than forty years in ministry with the Church of the Nazarene, I have often been asked: *"How does God speak to us?"* Most often, it's through His Word, prayer, or circumstances that leave no doubt. Sometimes it's the gentle whisper of the Holy Spirit that presses so strongly that it's not an "I think," but an "I know." And on some occasions, God speaks audibly. That has happened to me four times—and each time it changed my life.

In 1984, while driving on the interstate toward Birmingham, Alabama, as a young Christian, I suddenly heard my name called so clearly that I had to pull over. After searching through the car and finding nothing, I finally asked, *"Lord, is that You?"* In that moment, I experienced a powerful encounter with *The Voice*, telling me to visit an elderly woman I knew as a boy. He wanted me to tell her that she needed the Lord.

Initially, the woman rejected Him, and I even pleaded with her to change. Soon after, she fell into a coma, and when she woke, she asked for me. It was a moment that ultimately led her to finding Christ. It changed both of our lives (as she passed away eight weeks later). That day I followed God's voice, and it's forever etched in my memory.

The Voice in Hidden Creek is a fictional story, but its truth is real. Every believer who has ever asked, *"What does God want me to do, and how will I know?"* will find hope in these pages. This book took me fifteen years to write, and I believe every part of that journey was guided by the Lord.

My prayer is that these words inspire you, surprise you, and draw you closer to the One whose voice still speaks today—if you are willing to listen.

Chapter 1
Rotten Apples

Small town...itus. That's what it was. Plain, simple, and downright hidden, nestled in the wooded hills of Eastern Tennessee, resided a tiny area called Creek. Few outsiders knew of it, and those who did joked about it being a place called "Nowhere." No one knew the real story of how the town came into being. Some compared it to a weed that just popped up one day.

It was a place of mystery, producing many stories—some true, some rumors—of haunts and disappearing bodies. Vagrants rarely ventured into the area, and when they did, they were promptly run out of town, usually beaten or never to be seen again. Still, Creek had the beginnings of growth through rugged families who stuck out the difficult times and refused to give in to failure. Families lived with dreams—aspirations of making a life, building schools, churches, and commerce.

Most were farmers who grew corn, beans, and tobacco crops, while others developed supporting aspects of the farming business. Since the late 1920s, Creek had struggled to exist, but like most small communities, it pushed onward, growing and declining, and eventually established its identity, making a dot on the state map.

Sarvenson Mercantile and Hardware stood at the heart of the town as the most recognizable structure, serving not only as a center for goods and hardware but also as a makeshift gas station and tractor repair shop. It was the oldest building in Creek, dating back to the early 1910s, and sat on a prominent spot on the main unnamed road. Built from logs harvested from the heavily wooded area, the store displayed the ruggedness of early settlers. Huge gouges on the entryway scarred mainly by knife-throwing competitions exposed the fact that it was a local stamping ground. Several handmade rockers lined the front for the patrons to relax in or rock with the mountain breeze.

A large creaking door with five iron rings attached led the way inside. It was rumored that a man was once strapped to the door and shot for stealing from Sarvenson's, a tale which many locals held to be true because of its owner—Elijah Sarvenson—a massive bearded man of great height and brawn, with a short-fused temper, who on occasion had knocked the front door off the hinges into the street. And if he alone was not enough to handle any problems or complaints, his five equally large sons did. Each one, a lumberjack by trade.

Inside the store, there were impressive antler racks of whitetail deer nailed to every section of the wall in a kind of hodgepodge fashion. One near the entrance, with numerous points, was used for a hatrack. A sizeable fireplace, which kept the place warm during the bitter winter months, constructed from the stone of Massey River, graced the back of the store. Nearby, a square, hand-crafted table sat hewn out on the top, with a checkerboard pattern carved into its surface, where the locals played games and told lies. Since the passing of Elijah Sarvenson's wife, goods lay haphazardly all over the store, but he really did not care, seeing that his was the only mercantile store in twenty-five miles.

On the other hand, Morton's Feed and Seed down Main Street about a half mile, although small in comparison to Sarvenson, was perhaps the busiest store in Creek, seeing how it provided the most needed commodity at the time. Matthew Morton, a small balding man, was the proprietor. He was well-liked by almost everyone because of his unusual caring personality, fueled by his church upbringing to treat others as he would want to be treated. He gave credit to families who struggled, found work for those seeking employment, and always had a large candy jar in his office to share with the children of the town. Some of the unruly patrons of Creek, however, on occasion, took advantage of his kindness and size to take whatever they wanted, which they could not do with Sarvenson and his sons.

Without a vindictive spirit, Morton prayerfully took every setback, believing that the Lord would provide, and one day He would bring His righteous judgement. His greatest joy in life, and every parent in town knew it, was teaching children's Sunday School at the only church in Creek—Mount Ridge Baptist Church.

Beautiful and conflicting with the hardness of everyday life in Creek, Mount Ridge Baptist graced the area with the only colorful building in town. Painted gloss white with maroon trim, the church contrasted greatly with the rest of the town in appearance, and wildflowers sprouting during the spring in a field at the rear only added to the disparity. The high-pointed steeple, pointing like the finger of God, appeared out of place, belonging to a more northeastern setting of the United States. Inside, the oak pews were arranged in parallel rows on a shiny hardwood floor, and a lone upright piano, desperately needing tuning, sat front left. Stained glass images, carefully installed in place of the upper window sections, refracted various saints and biblical scenes, giving the place a warm glow.

Being the eighth pastor in seven years, Reverend Elden Winters, added to the warmth. A kind and caring man by nature, he was firm and grounded when needed. He was the first pastor whom mischief-makers could not run off or discourage from having revival meetings—and revival meetings he loved. Every six months, Elden would invite a traveling horseback evangelist to preach to his congregation like there was no tomorrow. Some meetings lasted a week, while some persisted for several weeks. Many of these traveling preachers were threatened, beaten, and dragged out of Creek by their own horse for preaching too much conviction for the roughnecks. One preacher in particular, who rode a magnificent white horse, was stomped right outside the front door of the church. Both his legs and numerous ribs were severely broken, nearly killing him.

Outside the church was a lone well with a screeching crank, offering a drink to whoever wanted one. On its crossbeam, Pastor Winters had nailed a sign with a message to reemphasize the gospel message: *"Let him who is thirsty, come and drink."* And drink they did... across the street.

Nowhere in Creek could there be more riffraff on any given day or time than at Samson's Saloon. The place was a stark contrast to Mount Ridge Baptist, reeking of strong drink, bad language, gambling, and numerous fights. It was as if Heaven and Hell were less than forty yards apart. "Sooner" Redman, a bartender and a despicably gruff man, ran the place and refereed the nightly brawls, which he allowed because he felt it brought business. It was to him a jab to the holier-than-thou minister across the way. Sooner had one helper on hand, Ian Swanner, to sweep, clean, and repair damages daily. He also doubled as the town casket builder because of his carpentry skills.

The history of Samson's Saloon could only be enlightened by Elijah Sarvenson when he was in a good mood, which was rare. The story reveals a moonshiner by the name of Jessie Samson, a brutal man who, according to Elijah, sent more men to their graves than he could count among the living. Elijah informed the townsfolk that Jessie Samson personally killed more than fifty men back in the early days of Creek and had a deep-seated hatred for women and preachers who interfered with his business of distributing moonshine to his customers.

He built the saloon with his own hands and served regular whiskey and beer out front, while moonshine flowed in the back. Elijah had reported that absolutely no one dared to cross Samson's path, and they all believed him, given the awe in his deep voice when he told them about the Samson tales. Samson, in an ironic fashion, met his end at the hands of a ninety-five-pound Alabama woman who shot him seven times for killing her husband with bad liquor. At about this time, the long arm of Federal Marshals began to force an end to the moonshine business, but funnily enough, the operation never stopped at Samson's.

Lightning. White Lightning. Corn Squeezin's. Moonshine. Copper flush. Whatever name fit now, it flowed in and out of the Creek community through Samson's. The problem of making moonshine had grown so out of control that outside federal law enforcement found it difficult to stop. As soon as one moonshine still was destroyed, another would pop up in its place, sometimes the same day. Several feds came up missing, feared, and, rightly so, dead. In a period of ten years, six officers were never seen or heard from again. After fighting a losing battle, the federal raids began to decrease, but the moonshiner outfits pressed on with batch after batch, remaining on constant alert and wary of all strangers who tried to venture too close.

Chapter 2
Berry Picking

Lila, Moses, and little Morris Wilson, a sharecropping family in their early thirties, hummed in perfect harmony to the old struggle and temptation songs from the past. They were steadily picking blackberries in a patch they found four miles north of Creek.

Their day started before sunrise with them consuming a quick breakfast of grits and sausage gravy, followed by a three-mile hike to the berry patch, pulling Sally, their faithful but slow mule. She was loaded with buckets to carry their gathering of berries for the day.

In their spare time, which was scarce—since survival is a full-time job—the Wilson family collected items from nature to help make ends meet. At the end of a long, hot day of picking berries, they usually made ten cents per bucket at a small, makeshift produce stand near Mount Ridge Baptist Church. An entire day's work usually yielded about one dollar and fifty cents.

Lila Wilson, a woman of grace, politeness, and a bright smile, was deeply loved by her family and neighbors. As an act of kindness, many times, she would hold out one bucket of berries to make cobblers for families facing worse conditions than her own. She had a joyous personality, full of laughter, and a face that could brighten up a room. Her relevance to the other sharecropper families could not be overlooked, as she was one of the rare people in the shanty region who could read. For little to nothing, she taught the basic elements of schooling to all the children and even to adults when time was on their side.

Additionally, Lila was also the spiritual leader of the area, as sharecropper families were not allowed to attend the white Mount Ridge Baptist Church in town. In response, she set up a small meeting house in a large barn to hold services. Most of the songs sung were from memory, and testimonies remained the highlight of the meetings. After which, Lila would lay hold of her tattered and worn Bible, reading the Word of God to the people. Even amid the adverse conditions, Lila's enthusiasm lifted the people's spirits, while she encouraged them to find the greatest spirit lifter—God Himself.

The couple always did the picking while young Morris, the Wilson's only child, stood nearby holding the reins of Sally and swatting flies attracted to the mule. At five years of age, he had the responsibility of guiding the mule along the edge of the patch as his parents picked and poured into larger buckets draped over Sally. Morris was a quiet boy, very respectful and obedient to his parents in every way. His clothes, adequate but worn, fit about two sizes too big for him, and he had a rope cinched tight about his waist to hold up his pants. The shoes he wore were in tatters, with frayed edges and holes that exposed the worn-out soles. Yet, they were the only pair he possessed, and he felt blessed to have them, considering most of his friends would go walking around barefoot.

His mother was the only school teacher he would ever have, and she had already taught him the ABCs, how to recognize words, and do simple arithmetic problems. What Morris enjoyed most, however, was his mother reading to him at night from the Bible. Snuggled underneath a thick homemade blanket and watching the candle beside his bed flicker, his mother opened his mind to the stories of David and Goliath, Daniel and the lion's den, and the Apostle Paul suffering a shipwreck. It was another world to young Morris... a world of victory and hope.

Morris's father taught him different lessons—life lessons. Tall, lean, strong, and spiritual, Moses worked hard to support his family. His life consisted of endless hours of preparing, planting, harvesting, and delivering crops for Mr. Davenport, a well-to-do man with a large farm east of Creek. There were over forty workers on the Davenport farm. However, due to Moses's work ethic, he gained the respect of the Davenport family and was put in charge of the entire operation. Still, Moses worked just like the rest in the dirt, in the heat, and in the rain.

During the winter months, Moses spent most of his time teaching Morris how to hunt for game, such as deer, squirrel, and rabbit. Morris discovered that during a specific time frame of the winter, a male deer's neck swells during the rut, and the buck creates a scrape line—a sporadic path of digs in the ground or rubs on trees forming a line through the woods for willing does to find him. It's also a sure way for a hunter to track the buck.

Moses also shared with Morris that the best time to squirrel hunt is during a gentle drizzle. Not only did the light rain make the squirrels become more active, but it also dampened the leaves so Morris could walk quietly through the woods. After each hunting session, Morris was required to clean the only gun the Wilson family possessed, a small-caliber rifle.

One of the sayings from Moses that always lingered in Morris's mind was, *"If you don't take care of what you have, you'll never have anything."*

There are other sayings his father had given him—some practical, some sobering. Moses repeatedly told him about being cautious in the white man's world, yet to respect each person, white or otherwise, if respect is due. And to do as the Good Book said, *"You shall love your neighbor as yourself."* Doing that alone, according to Moses, would make the world a much better place.

THE SUN SEARED everything in its path with its hot, high-noon rays. Morris pulls out his checkered handkerchief—one his mother had made from his patched overalls—to wipe the beading sweat on his forehead. In the process, he catches a whiff of something sweet wafting in the air.

"Momma... I smell something good!" he declares with excitement, as the sausage, grits, and gravy from breakfast begin to wear off.

"Now hush, honey," she chides. "You had your breakfast, which is more than what most folks have had today." Then she resumes picking.

Moses abruptly quits picking, and it catches Lila's attention. He, too, smells the same aroma, and it's all too familiar. Beads of sweat begin to pour more rapidly down his face, which now wears an expression of fear. His heart races. Guilt and remorse wash over him immediately as he thinks about the predicament he may have created for his family. The thought paralyzes him as it flashes across his mind, *Shine making! And close by!*

Gathering his feelings and trying to think clearly and cautiously, he motions for Lila to be quiet and not make any sudden motions. He reaches for Sally's reins and lifts Morris onto her back, patting his head as if simply giving the boy a rest. Handing the reins to Lila, Moses continues picking berries, though only a small amount this time. Then, with a calm sense of control, he, Lila, Morris, and Sally ease away, careful to look as though they're just finishing for the day.

Moses hopes that if they slip away quietly, without drawing attention, perhaps—though it's a big maybe—anyone watching might just let them leave peacefully. So far, the plan seems to work. They make it one hundred yards back toward home. Everything is going to be okay, or so he thought.

But lookouts Will Gilmore (a greasy-haired man in his forties with numerous scars on his face) and Jake Tanner (a maniac on two legs) spot them. Their suspicious, guided movements tip off the men. The group below must have discovered the operation, they assume. Bored from inactivity since the last federal agent they strung up a year ago, the two perk up, ready to confront the suspects.

Gilmore flashes his mirror an exact number of times to alert the other gang members. He signals Forrest Driscoll, son of the notorious Samuel Driscoll (ramrod of major stills in Eastern Tennessee) and "No Good Tucker," as they wait on a hillside that leads out of the area.

Meanwhile, Jake, having loaded his rifle, raises it to fire until Gilmore sees him and shoves the gun away.

"What do you think you're doing? We want to get them all... see! If you kill one, the other two may get away. And you know what happens to us if they squeal to the feds. Old man Driscoll would have our heads!"

"Ah, come on! Just let me shoot 'em! I know I can git 'em from here!" snorts Jake.

Gilmore snatches the gun away and cracks him across the head with the butt. Wincing in pain, Jake stares back angrily as blood trickles from his ear. *I hate getting paired with this crazy nut,* Gilmore mutters under his breath.

Still, they have a job to do, and Gilmore fears Samuel Driscoll far more than he fears Jake Tanner. And so both men mount their horses and race down the hillside, pushing branches aside in a frantic descent.

At this moment, Moses is seriously bothered. Out of the corner of his eye, he thinks he saw a signal flash. He hopes it's just light reflecting from a rock, but his instincts say otherwise. He has only one concern: getting his family to safety.

Unable to stand the pressure any longer, Moses flings the berry buckets from Sally, grabs Lila, throws her and Morris onto the mule, and slaps Sally hard on the backside. The mule lurches forward into a fast trot over a grassy knoll and toward a stand of trees—only to come face-to-face with "No Good Tucker," who fires a shot into the air.

The sound becoming too much for the old mule to take, she begins to buck and bray furiously, tossing Lila and Morris to the ground with a hard thump. Confused and dazed, they both crawl around in the grass, trying to get their bearings while, at the same time, staying away from their faithful mule's kicks.

Moses's thoughts race as he runs toward them in desperation. *If all of us are going to die, I'm not going down without trying.* Every step feels like a milestone... time slows... closer... closer... and then— pain. An awful pain.

A bullet rips through his left thigh, sending him crashing to the ground. Gritting his teeth, Moses rises to his knees, then to his feet. He pushes forward, but another bullet strikes his right shoulder, and he crashes again.

"Going somewhere, boy?" Gilmore calls out, perched thirty yards away on his horse. "Wouldn't recommend you gettin' up again... or else the next one goes in your head."

Moses lies still, panting, gasping for air, his mind searching for a way out. In that dire moment, all that came to his mind was what his God-fearing grandmother had told him time after time.

"When all else fails, put your faith in the Good Lord. He always has a plan and purpose for everything. If the situation is good, praise him. If bad, praise him more. Ours is not to question, but to obey. The Lord works things out for those who love him. And above all, honor the Lord in life and in death because He will not forget his own."

Moses lifts his bloody hand toward Heaven in praise.

But Gilmore sees it as defiance. He charges forward, tosses a rope around Moses's raised arm, and drags him toward the other group.

At the same time, Tucker, a hulky man with a bushy beard, grabs Lila by her hair, yanking her to the ground. She screams in pain from the abuse he inflicted, while desperately trying to locate her son, who had crawled away from the chaotic scene. Tucker flings Lila one last time onto her back, knocking the breath out of her.

Just then, Gilmore pulls Moses up next to his wife. Lila, upon seeing her husband, screams in horror at his condition—bloody, scratched, and half dead. The lookouts had arrived as Driscoll and Tanner rode up to them, creating a long and tense silence. Moses lay still, and Lila could barely breathe, while the four men glare menacingly at the scene.

Finally, Samuel Driscoll, the leader of the mob, rides in and breaks the silence.

"What'chaw doin' up here?" he growls, spitting tobacco at Moses's face.

"Nothin' but pickin' berries," Moses replies, wincing in pain. He knew they were in a life-and-death situation. He felt sure he was a goner, but hoped they might let his family go free.

"Berries!" snorts Driscoll. "You see any berries, Jake?"

Baring all his rotten teeth, Jake Tanner shakes his head with an evil smile. "Nope! No berries 'round here! All I see is a pack of liars! No good snoopin' liars!"

"Honestly, we were just picking berries," cries Lila through her tears. "We didn't come lookin' for trouble, we—"

Lila did not get to finish her statement, as she was interrupted by a kick to her chest by Driscoll. "Hush, woman! And keep your trap shut!" Driscoll growls. "I'm talking to your man only... you understand?" Turning to Moses, he repeated his question, "Now I ask you again... what are ya'll doin' up here!"

Before Moses could answer, Jake Tanner cries out in a shrill, almost hysterical voice, "Pickin' berries! Pickin' berries! Pickin' berries! Watch the liar say pickin' berries! Bet he's one of them do-gooder people! Christ...ians!" Tanner spat as he says the word "Christians" as if it left a bitter taste in his mouth.

"Liars! Liars! All of them are liars! Pickin' berries!" He continues snickering and laughing insanely. Tanner's insanity was apparent. Most of the shiners ignored his antics, the snickering, evil laughter, the crowing at sunrise, and the squawking at sundown, mainly because he was one of the best marksmen in Tennessee, and the fact that he had escaped an insane asylum.

Tucker despised Tanner and couldn't stand to be paired with him. Tanner's psychotic antics irritated his nerves, and seeing how he had everyone's attention only annoyed him even more. Striding over, Tucker backhands Tanner and demands that he keep quiet. Tanner rolls around on the ground, then crawls a short distance, and begins to snicker once more about berries.

Moses and Lila cling to one another, trembling as the reality of the trouble begins to sink in. In resignation, they bowed their head, and *"Trust in the Lord..."* began echoing through Lila's mind.

"How many times have I told others... to trust in the Lord?"

Moses, on the other hand,was thinking about the story of Joshua and the words, *"Be strong and courageous."*

The sound of a snapped branch broke their moment of meditation. Looking up, they see Morris peeking from behind a tree.

"Morris! Run, Morris! Run!" the couple yells with all their strength, bracing themselves for the repercussions.

At the sound of their voice, Morris makes tracks into the woods as fast as his five-year-old feet could carry him. Darting through the trees, he felt as if the Devil himself was chasing him. His heart raced, sweat stinging his eyes. At that moment, all he could think about was the growing distance between him and his family, and whether he would ever see them again.

"The boy!" Tanner screams. "He's gettin' away!"

"Let him go!" Driscoll orders. "He's just a runt. We'll catch him later. Right now, we must decide what to do with these two."

Jake Tanner turns his attention back to the captives, with a smirk creeping across his face. Pain and suffering gave him an adrenaline rush, making him more and more excited as the minutes went by.

"What are we goin' to do with 'em?" questions Driscoll. "What would Pa Driscoll do with these so-called innocent berry pickers?"

"Hang 'em high!" huffs Jake with an evil laugh. Imitating that he had a rope around his neck, he dances side to side, shuffling his feet faster and faster, then, falling as if dead to the ground.

"Tucker, what about you?" asked Driscoll.

"Hang 'em!"

"Gilmore?" piped the leader.

"String 'em up!"

"It's unanimous then!" pronounces Driscoll, looking like a judge who had hammered the gavel for the verdict.

Tanner hysterically jumps around like the madman he is. He grabs a large rope from his horse, running it back and forth through his hands, nearly peeling his own skin. He races to a nearby oak at the edge of the field and throws both ends over and then pulls them through the remaining loop. He had made two nooses from the one piece of rope. All the while, he was spouting vile things and the importance of a good knot.

Gilmore and Tucker tie Moses's and Lila's hands behind their backs and guide them over to the tree where the maniacal Tanner stood. Driscoll rounds up Sally, who was now grazing as if nothing was happening. He helps Tanner hoist Lila and Moses onto the old mule's back.

Driscoll pushes back his hat, showing what remains of matted hair from his already balding head. Pulling out a fresh plug of tobacco, he settles in to wait, spitting occasionally. He wanted Jake to soak in every second of the hanging, knowing that it would ultimately pacify his totally insane partner.

After a long while, he sternly asks, "Any last words?"

Side by side, they bow their heads and whisper prayers aloud. Lila prays. Moses prays.

"Ain't no God gonna help ya'll now," shaking his head.

Tanner snickers. Driscoll slaps the mule.

Chapter 3
Hidden Creek High

Wind whistled through the massive old oaks lining the pathway to the entrance of Hidden Creek High School, creating a bizarre, eerie sound that ripped leaves of gold, red, and yellow shades from the branches. It was raining the color of autumn against the relatively blue sky.

Out on the front lawn, brilliant harvest decorations made up of hay, corn, pumpkins, and stalks were artfully placed around a rustic prairie wagon, giving the school a traditional charm that imaged the celebrations of Tennessee during the month of October. In a rather large oval center court, two ancient oaks were surrounded by a small white picket fence with a gate that led to park benches and a massive flagpole, which was now clanging its rope in rhythm with the wind. Leading up to the front step, well-kept, trimmed hedges lined every walkway, and grayed, flowerless rose bushes clung to metal grates mounted to the side of the building where banners were tied proclaiming the next victim of the football season.

Built in 1942, shortly after the community of Creek was incorporated and renamed Hidden Creek, the school, with its red brick exterior and colonial columns, exhibited a picture of academia and southern flavor found in its Tennessee heritage. It was a purely secular school in that, like every other school in the state, it followed the same strict guidelines of the *Separation of Church and State*. Originally founded on Christian principles in 1942, the school at that time had daily prayer, teaching of the Bible, and Christocentric Christmas programs. However, in sharp contrast, today there were no prayers, no Bibles allowed, and no mention of Christ during Christmas celebrations. Nevertheless, the school served a significant purpose in the community and was rich in historical background.

And what a history! The school served as an emergency bomb shelter during the World War II era and later became a hot dancing spot for the bop of the 1950s. It survived the turbulent sixties and had a disruptive time incorporating integration. The structure had also weathered three fires and numerous tornado alerts over the years, and basically still remained the way it was when it was first built. The only additions were a new gym, a country-type football field in the back with concrete bleachers, and a more modern concession stand, which served everything from hot dogs to boiled peanuts.

Football was king in Hidden Creek, as with most small communities in the 1990s. It was the talk of the town year-round, and Coach Red Holiday held the demanding position as head coach, where one week he could be a genius, and the next, a complete half-wit to local armchair and bleacher coaches. Although he produced winning seasons and people loved his "get tough or die" approach on the field, he was miserable internally. His secret desire was to leave what he called "Hicksville" and take over a large 5A program in Nashville with all the benefits and trimmings. His win-or-die attitude toward football had already cost him his wife and family, who now lived in North Carolina. Age was also becoming a factor in his resume. For extra money, Coach Holiday also taught eleventh-grade history (if it could be called that). All the students loved his class because it was considered as one of the "breeze" classes among the student body, consisting of just enough history, meaningless discussions, jokes, and, of course, football. Once on that subject, the class was technically over.

THE BELL RANG, instigating an explosion of motion and excitement in the hallway of Hidden Creek High, lined with banners for the upcoming game with Warsaw High, last year's winner of the 1A division. Through the mayhem, a tennis ball ricocheted off the wall, narrowly missing several pupils, and paper airplanes soared and floated in various locations. Books echoed a hollow thud as they found their resting place in the back of the lockers. Quick slams of metal doors confirmed the student's hasty desire to leave the building and their books. It was Friday, and that meant a weekend of freedom. First on the agenda was the night's football game, where anybody from anywhere showed up at Hidden Creek's Sarvenson Stadium—named after some old guy whose identity was unknown by most of the kids.

After the game, it was a mad race down Main Street to Mooky's—a local burger hangout that made the best grilled burgers, curly fries, and milkshakes in the area. Mooky's was lit up with bright green neon arches, drive-in order aisles, and an inside eating area with a 1950s-style decor. By ten o'clock, the place would be rocking with activity, of hot rod cars, loud stereos, and of course, great food. Saturday, if not a repeat at Mooky's, most of the teens went to THC Drive-In, a worn but still functioning theater, with their dates for the latest movies. And Sunday, well, that was a different story.

Sunday was to be a day of rest and a day of worship. Almost

everyone in Hidden Creek understood the "rest" part, but worship in a church wasn't high on the docket for most Hidden Creek students. Taking on the ideas and feelings of their parents, church was a crutch, a place of gossip, a den of cliques, and a waste of time. Besides, numerous sports programs on television took priority, and when nothing was interesting on television, swimming, fishing, and other activities filled the void. Furthermore, it was not in any way "cool" to be religious. Teens who were dragged into going to church by their parents were either viewed with sympathy, harassed, or left out of the mix of social circles.

Ben Walker, who was a senior, stood out from the crowd, though. His tall, blond, athletic, and handsome features spoke volumes to the dreamy-eyed girls who overlooked his dedication to Community Church and his commitment to Christ. As if his looks alone were not enough, Ben was the star receiver on the Hidden Creek Badger Football Team. He was rewriting the record books in receptions, yards gained, and touchdowns. He had attracted interest from the University of Tennessee for a scholarship not only in sports but also for his impressive grades.

Ben did volunteer work around the school during the summer months when not practicing football, and helped out at the mission store, distributing goods to needy families.

Ben's religious dedication and success cost him, however, on various fronts. He had few male friends, with the rest being jealous of his looks and athletic nature, which drove several of them to dislike Ben altogether. The only ones who respected him—though not for his religious attitude—were his teammates on the football team. When it came to the young women around him, it was a different ball game. He rarely stayed out beyond his curfew of eleven o'clock, even on weekends. He didn't experiment with drugs or alcohol, and had a strict, well-known commitment around campus of saving himself until marriage. These reasons alone had cost him several dates, but it was his reminding invitations to church that really drove them crazy and kept the young ladies at a distance. Still, Ben was a hunk...

Adriana Peterson, Samantha Rice, and JoAnn Mobley—all juniors—were standing at the end of the hall, giggling and whispering in soft tones. Their mouths were somewhat hidden by the books in their hands. After a glance down the hall, they begin to squeal again. Their target was none other than Ben Walker, who was strolling toward the office.

"He is soooo... cute!" remarks Adriana, as she drags out the word *"so."*

"Bet I could change his ways," Samantha says with a mischievous smile plastered on her face. "I have ways. He wouldn't stand a chance if he were in my hands for long."

"Bet you couldn't even get him to kiss you!" snaps JoAnn. "I heard he won't even kiss on the first date. I wouldn't mind that as long as it happened on the second. I heard he is quite a gentleman too... opening doors, saying thank you, and all that. I wonder who he's planning to take to the prom next spring... maybe me!"

"Not if I have something to do with it," Samantha says with a smirk, giggling sheepishly again as Ben reappears in the hallway. Adriana and JoAnn, upon seeing him, join in the subdued titter.

The three girls nearly jumped out of their skins when a commanding voice thundered through their conversations.

"What are you still doing here?" demands Maggie Stewart with drill sergeant authority. "Don't you know the buses are about to leave? Either get out there, or you'll have to walk home."

The three juniors slam their lockers and leave in a hurry, peering over their shoulders to get one final look at Ben Walker. Giggling one last time, they chatter in a whisper as they exit through the hall doors.

Maggie Stewart, an attractive office secretary in her late thirties, took a deep breath. It had been a long week, and the weekend didn't look promising. She still had a lot of work to do around the house, taking care of the dishes, washing clothes, and shopping. And she had to do it all alone. As she walked down the long hall, her mind wandered.

I was once like them... a giggling girl secretly dreaming of a cute young man who would sweep me away and make my dreams come true. To feel his strong hand hold mine... to touch his lips with a passionate kiss and experience those light, butterfly feelings of young love... to have my world spinning around my man. My man. And now, look at me. Living alone with a dog and a lazy cat, and having to work with the witch who created this mess that I'm in. Thirteen years of marriage down the drain, and nothing to show for it but pain... just pain. All because of some foolish rumor. Why did it have to happen to me? Why me? Lost in her thoughts and completely forgetting about her surroundings, Maggie accidentally bumps into Principal Tyrel "Ty" Walker as she steps into the office, spilling her soft drink all over his finest suit coat.

"Oh, I'm sorry!" Maggie cries, reaching for the roll of paper towels near the sink, wiping quickly to keep the stain from worsening.

"How clumsy of me! I can't believe I did—"

Ty responds with a smile. "Don't worry, Maggie. It'll come out. I needed to send this coat to the cleaners anyway. You just helped me along."

His gentle manners instantly calmed her fears. Ty Walker had that way about him. He was perhaps the most respected man around Hidden Creek, and being a capable principal for the last five years had only increased that honor. Forty-five years old, six-feet-four, and very distinguished in every aspect of education, personality, and looks, Ty Walker was exactly what the school needed after the horrible accident of the last principal, killed by a drunk driver over in the neighboring town of Sipley.

Ty's popularity prompted several Hidden Creek City Council members to goad him to toss his hat in the ring of politics, but Ty refused politely again and again, stating that politics belonged to politicians, of which he was not. His main goal, his calling, was steering and directing young adults in the pursuit of education.

"I'm going to pay your bill," Maggie says as she continues wiping Ty's shirt.

"It's fine, Maggie." In an attempt to stop the assault on his coat, Ty reaches for her hand, indicating that she should stop.

"You're sure?"

"Absolutely sure."

"I could take your coat to the cleaners for you, and…" she insisted with a worried frown on her face.

"Maggie! Don't worry," Ty chides.

At precisely the wrong moment, Nettie Driscoll, school coordinator and town gossip—and not necessarily in that order— walks in and catches Ty still holding Maggie's hands. Giving them both a smirk of suspicion, she stored the "juicy scene" for future reference.

Nettie Driscoll is a woman in her late thirties, slightly overweight, with dyed reddish-brown hair that adds color to her somewhat attractive appearance. In terms of work efficiency, none was better, but as an individual, she was in a class of her own, unequaled by her persistence in keeping the dirt on everyone and anything in town. Usually, the news was destructive in nature. Entire families in town refused to speak to one another. Feelings were wounded and never healed, and proportionally, divorce was a prospering venue in Hidden Creek and the surrounding areas because of her. So much so that she earned the nickname "Terminator," which many in town angrily snarled under their breath behind her back. Very few people would talk to her because of her twisting way with words.

"Well, well...," she says, looking like a shark that found blood. "What is going on here behind closed doors? Hmm... I leave you two alone just for a second and come in to find this?"

Maggie lurches forward to attack Nettie, but Ty immediately stops her.

Nettie was the primary provoker in Maggie's divorce from her ex-husband, Marshall, through her manipulative ways. Maggie disliked the "witch" so much that she tried to think of ways to get rid of her. But whenever she came up with the perfect plan, something inside of her pulled her back to reality and told her not to.

"Just an accident, Nettie," Ty replies, letting go of Maggie's hands.

"Just an accident, huh? That is what they all say, and before you know it—"

Before Nettie finished her thought, Ty interjected with a gentle but firm voice.

"Nettie, now I've warned you about starting rumors. They will come back to haunt you, and I don't want to see you get hurt."

"I know. I know," replies Nettie, trying not to listen to him.

She hurries to her office, ignoring the conversation. Ty Walker had a way of bringing conviction to her. Practically everyone in town hated her, except for good old Christian Ty. After her hysterectomy operation, Ty was the only one who came to visit, and year after year, he was the only one who sent her birthday, Christmas, or even Valentine's Day cards. He once picked up the bill for her car repair during a time she was struggling financially.

Yes, Ty Walker was an unusual man, loving the unloved. This

made Nettie very uncomfortable because she did not understand love herself.

Watching Nettie leave, Maggie takes a deep breath in response to her true feelings. Scurrying back to her desk, she removes her purse and says nothing. Her face, however, tells the whole story of an inward pain eating at her, raging in her soul, and not finding peace. Nettie Driscoll is a thorn in her side that hurts deeply. As Maggie turns to depart for the day, she stops and blurts out, "Oh, Ty," as if remembering something.

"Yes, Maggie," relieved that Maggie wanted to talk.

"That son of yours is creating a stir in the hearts of half the girls on campus. We are going to have to place crossing guards wherever he goes," she says jokingly.

"Ben can't help what he inherited from his mother," grinned Ty.

Looking at how handsome Ty Walker is, Maggie thinks to herself, *That is just like him… to give credit to someone else.*

Around the back of the school, Moe Wilson, a gentle and deeply religious black man, was seen walking from his shop across a weathered basketball court, starting his security checks on the rear doors, just as he had done for the past thirty-seven years.

Moe had put in a long day as groundskeeper and custodian, performing his regular duties: cleaning, sweeping, and mopping, and he didn't mind. It was always an honor for him to hear people comment on how well-kept the school was and how beautiful the grounds were. It was an even greater honor to serve his Lord and his God. The verse that stuck with him daily was, "If a man will not work, let him not eat…," which was posted in his office.

After checking all the doors, Moe heads to the shed, swings the large doors together, and snaps the lock shut.

The sky was darkening with the lateness of the day, and the wind was relentless as Moe struggled against it across a grassy field. He tucked his weathered hands into his tattered but warm coat, with his mind wandering to the warm fire he planned to build in his small, although adequate home, not far from the school. He licked his lips, fantasizing over the cup of hot chocolate and imagining himself snuggling down beside the fire to read his Bible, pray, and get a good night's rest.

Walking briskly down the path leading home, Moe begins to hum an old familiar tune he had learned from many years past. The act of humming and praying while he walked always had a way to relax and encourage his soul, so much so that townsfolk had nicknamed him "hummer." Some of the more despicable ones called him "berry picker" as an insult from the past.

Although he owned an old pickup, he enjoyed walking and rarely drove. Walking saved him money and was more enjoyable because it gave him time to pray and to hum.

Walking faster now, Moe heads down Dove Street as he nears his house, groping in his pocket for his keys when they suddenly fall through a hole in his coat. As he bends over to retrieve them, a strong gust of wind nearly topples him. Moe grows still, as he begins to tremble, not from the cold, but from a strong presence he can feel.

His eyes widen as he looks towards the Heavens, and a bright glow fills his face, as if he has seen an angelic vision. Moe instantly drops to his knees and begins worshipping God with every fiber of his being. The words spilling from his lips repeatedly:

"It has come... Praise be to you, Lord. It has finally come."

Chapter 4
Family

For Ty Walker, nothing was as soothing as the late evening drive home to Cinnamon Lane. It gave him time to reflect on the day, his ups and downs, victories, and mistakes. As principal of Hidden Creek, it was easy for someone to find fault with something he did or didn't do.

That is what leadership is... to lead people, and then let them find fault. Ty smiled at that concept, and how ironic it was as he turned onto Main Street deep in thought. *People want to be led, but they want to pull their reins the way they see fit. I wonder if that's how God feels about us. We want Him to lead us, but we are holding the reins, telling Him which way to go or what to do.*

Ty's mind continues to drift. *Poor Maggie... I know she is so hurt. It hurts me to see her that way. She has so much potential to be more than an office secretary... I must pray for her more.*

He turns onto Barrymore Street, where there are oaks of numerous colors lining both sides of the road. It is his favorite street; so peaceful, so beautiful, and enough to stimulate the weakest in faith to believe in God.

"God," Ty says out loud, turning the curve around Turner's Pond. But he did not hear God's response, even though it was a resounding, "YES."

Ty continues driving on Barrymore until he arrives at a new subdivision that has just been built. Lost in his thoughts and completely oblivious to his surroundings, he did not notice the two small boys ahead, riding bicycles in the yard.

"Tommy! Come on! Let's ride out here!" yells Bobby Gentry, cousin of Tommy Gentry, visiting for the weekend.

"Come on! It's no fun in the grass," he whines. There aren't any cars coming... I haven't seen many since I've been here."

"But we can't! My momma told us we are not supposed to go on the road," Tommy responds to him. We can ride here in the drive and the yard. Look, we can build a ramp here!"

"Momma's boy! Chicken! Auckkk, auckkk, auckkk," sneers Bobby, imitating a squawking chicken and flapping his arms.

"I am not!" Tommy defends himself, "I'll show you!"

In one leap, he mounts his bicycle and takes off, pedaling as fast as he can. Bobby, in his desire not to be left behind, follows carelessly, exiting the drive into Barrymore Street.

Too deep in thought, Ty had only seconds to react. The two boys came out of nowhere like a bad dream. Ty stomps on the brakes with both feet. The sound of screeching tires fills the air. Smoke billows from the back rubber of Ty's 1993 Roughrider, and all he could do was holler.

"Dear Jesus!" he cries out.

Sliding to a complete stop, he looks out the window and sees the two boys who have ridden back into the yard, tumbling down into a rough ditch. At this point, his heart is racing terribly as he instantly jumps out of his vehicle and runs toward Tommy and Bobby.

"Are you two alright?" Ty asks, panting with deep breaths.

"Oh yeah, we're fine," Bobby replies with pride in his voice. "Tommy skinned his arm, though."

"Are you sure you're okay?"

"Aw, yeah... tougher than he is!" Tommy sneers at his cousin.

Mrs. Gentry's worried and angry voice breaks into the conversation. "Tommy! Bobby! Get over here this instant! How many times have I warned you not to ride into the street? You could have gotten killed..."

She stops in her tracks, recognizing the presence of Principal Walker, clearly shaken, hands on his knees, with quivering breath.

"Mr. Walker, are you okay?"

"Fine, ma'am."

"I am so sorry these boys did this. They are going to get their behinds torn up for sure."

"I'm fine if they are." Ty replies, heading back to his car. He starts the engine, backs up slowly, and then eases on toward the direction he was originally headed.

"Now you two! Get in the house! Pick up those bikes... and don't leave them in the ditch! How many times have I told you about the road?" Mrs. Gentry huffs.

Grabbing their bikes, the two youngsters scurry toward the house, Bobby tugging at his pants to keep them from falling down. Their voices were heard above the sound of the slamming screen door, "But Momma, we were just..."

THE PHONE RINGS at the quiet home of Maggie Stewart, which makes Rotator bark furiously. Maggie emerges from the bathroom, muttering, "I'm coming..." and shuffles toward the phone, wearing a robe, all the while trying to get Rotator to hush. It was Friday night, and she didn't have a date or even want one, for that matter.

It is horrible being alone, rejected, and tossed aside. It was worse with no prospective companionship in sight. All that comforted her was cliff-hanging mysteries she checked out at the county library. They helped her forget her problems. Now, most likely, this was some telemarketer trying to sell her something she didn't need or, even worse, asking for donations to some fund. She always gave them a difficult time with this response, "That's what we pay taxes for."

"Hello," she answers, sounding frustrated, "this is Maggie."

The voice on the other end of the line makes her drop the phone, accidentally hitting Snoozer, her Siamese cat. He jolts out across the carpet on a dead run. She quickly picks up the phone, and huge tears well up in her eyes as the voice is not that of a stranger.

"Yes," she says, trembling, "I'm here."

TY DRIVES ON, still shaken by the near accident. It made him begin to contemplate once more. *How many times has God intervened when we were not aware? What about those two boys? How many times have my family and I been spared by God's providence? I know God is real and watches out for all of us. However, when is the decision made as to whether we live or die?*

Steering the Roughrider into the driveway, Ty notices his daughter Audrey playing tea party with a collection of stuffed animals through the large front window of their home. Audrey was serving her participants with ladylike precision in their make-believe tea and cookie time.

"How rapidly they grow up," whispers Ty, pulling up to the house.

Audrey is just five years old, but her behavior often belied her age, showcasing the true innocence of childhood. With her long, curly blonde hair, brown eyes, and full lips, she could easily pass for a cherub. However, it was her demeanor and character that fascinated many adults from the neighborhood and church. She developed a neighborhood giving box for needy children and was known for her polite and courteous mannerisms.

Her visits to Shady Oaks retirement home with her father, where she carried handpicked flowers, were always heartwarming, and her character was just so rare, especially for a group that can be so self-centered.

"Daddy!" Audrey hollers, hopping up and down as if ants were biting her toes as she sees her father.

Ty steps out of the car and into the reaching arms of his daughter, kisses her gently, and receives a loving bear hug around the neck. "Have a good day, honey?"

"Yes, sir! A very great day! Let's see... I had my bowl of Oogles cereal, some bacon, and my yummy juice for breakfast. Then I brushed my teeth and made my bed... well, Mommy helped me. Then I prayed for the kids who don't have anything. Then, we read some good books." She rattled out a long list of her day and then finally came to a pause with a sigh, "And I wish I could go to school with you."

"I know, honey. It will not be long." At that moment, Ty began to feel an inward aggravation for the foot-dragging by civic and local leaders on the issue of kindergarten in Hidden Creek. Next year, there would be K-4 and K-5, even if he had to start it in his own home.

"You have the best school teacher in the whole wide world right here at home."

"I know... but it would be better to go to the big school and learn all the great things that you know about, Daddy!"

"Well, what else have you done today?"

We went shopping. We looked at a lot of stuff. Then we went to

Mrs. Bishop's and had tea and cookies—the big chocolate chip ones! Then, we went to the market, and Mommy said she was tired." She concluded with her face showing concern.

"We have to help Mommy, don't we?" Ty rubs Audrey's hair and directs her to the kitchen. Ty was anxious to check on his wife, Laurie. At the age of thirty-nine, she ran a greater chance of losing their baby, and he could not bear that again. He knew the risks. The thought made him feel a cold chill go up his spine. He and Laurie had lost a previous child moments before birth. Something had gone wrong during the delivery process, and his would-be son never took his first breath.

Ty remembered the heaving sorrow as the doctors handed the lifeless infant to him and Laurie to hold and console. They believed that the moment would provide some kind of closure or help soothe the pain. And it was painful. Heart-wrenching pain. In fact, after the funeral, he recalled blaming God for the loss, and yet, later found that God was not at fault but had been there all along. It was an unhappy memory, but now, another child was only a few months away.

"Laurie?" Ty calls out in a stirred voice, not finding her in the kitchen.

"In here."

As he enters, he sees Laurie wrestling with several pillows on the living room couch. She obviously was having some difficulty arranging them to be comfortable.

"Here, let me help you."

"My back. Why is it always the back that hurts?" whined Laurie. She whisked back her blonde hair from across her face. It was lovely, long hair that hung with curls and she struggled to keep it with the southern humidity. Her facial features were strong and somewhat pointed with cute dimples and beautiful brown eyes. She was of average height and weight with one exception... the barrel, as she called it, at her waist, which now was becoming even more uncomfortable.

"Perhaps I could massage your back for you. Do you think that would help?"

"No. No. Nothing will help except rest." She lay back in utter exhaustion from the busy day. Ty had warned her not to overdo herself in activities, but she was an extrovert, and that further complicated matters. Laurie loved people and being on the go. This time, nevertheless, she wished that she had listened to the wisdom of her husband.

"Audrey told me of the busy day you two had."
"Yes... I know... I overdid myself again and I feel awful about not seeing Ben play tonight," hoping for compassion instead of a lecture. "Oh, by the way, Maggie Stewart called just before you came in and wants you to call her back. It sounded important. Any idea of what it is?"

"I have an idea. I suspect it is about today." Ty picks up the newspaper and glances at the headlines.

"Oh. Let me take a wild guess... Nettie!" pipes Laurie.

"Could be. We must pray for both. They both need the Lord."

"I cannot repeat what Mrs. Bishop said about what one of them needs, but she was obviously referring to Nettie. What is it going to take for Nettie to realize that she is destroying lives and making her own even more miserable?"

"Nettie must be shown love. That is the only thing that is going to change her. Love the unloved. That's what Jesus did, and so will we," Ty states, reaching for the phone.

Laurie turned on the television and battled with the pillows once more while Ty went into the kitchen to talk to Maggie. She could overhear bits and pieces of the conversation, but soon got lost in the program about bloopers on television. It took her mind off the nagging backache.

Ten minutes later, Ty hangs up with Maggie and joins Laurie on the couch to watch TV, while giving her neck a gentle rub. Not only did Laurie enjoy the neck rub, but also their time together.

"Is everything okay with Maggie?" Laurie questions as she turns off the television.

"Just fine, honey," he answers curtly as if he wanted to put an end to the questioning. Laurie, upon sensing this, took a pause, knowing that her husband preferred to keep some conversations private.

"Why don't you relax, and I'll get supper going?"

"Now, Ty... you have worked all day!"

"It's no problem. Just rest, please."

Ty turns on some soft music for Laurie and goes into the kitchen. Soon, the faint sound of pots and pans rattled, and the smell of polish sausage, fried potatoes, and green beans filled the air. And at the focal point of it all, Principal Tyrel Walker, the most respected man in all of Hidden Creek, was knee deep in dishes and preparing supper for the family. Pride was never an issue with him, while humility was. He found chores an honor, a blessing, and an example to the children, and he did everything out of love.

"Oh, how fortunate I am to have such a wonderful husband, sweet Lord..." whispers Laurie, reveling in the lively sounds of household activities.

Chapter 5
Voices

A blue neon light flickered from a bad ballast on the sign at Samson's bar, creating an eerie glow as dawn broke silently on the valley. The fog added to the scene as it flowed through town, trying to lift into the hills, lingering, as if reluctant to leave. Antique wrought iron streetlamps dimly cut through the fog, impersonating an old London horror movie with all the ghosts. And Hidden Creek had plenty of its own ghosts—unsolved murders, missing persons, divorce, and crime were just the tip of the iceberg. There were also haunts of prejudice, hatred, and strife with foundations fabricated by the founding fathers of the town that pulsed through the veins of numerous townsfolk.

Parked at Main and Little Valley Road, Officer Mac McMurphy settles his head against the seat rest of his squad car. He takes a long drag from his cigarette and sips some strong coffee he bought at the local Rip-N-Jip.

It had been a long night for the aging officer. First, he broke up a few altercations while policing the Hidden Creek High School football game with Warsaw High. Next, he arrested some small-timers who had a great desire to show their artistic skills on the side of City Hall. And as usual on Friday night, Mac hauls in "Greasy" Gilmore (alias town drunk) for the weekly ritual and caps the night off with a burglar break-in at 915 Willow Street.

Arriving at the house, it appears the residents are not home or out of town. Upon inspecting the premises, he finds some broken glass near the back door, and nothing else looks suspicious.

Glad there was a watchful neighbor at this hour. Probably scared off the burglar, he thought, as the feeling of relief gushed over him. Burglars usually panic when caught, and then, in intense situations, people get killed. And living—that's what he wanted to do.

Mac had three more months until he retired. Finally, after almost thirty-two years with the force, he felt like he had dealt with plenty of the small, but insane town. In those years, he had been shot twice, cut numerous times, run down by a hostile wife-beater in a souped-up four-wheel-drive pickup, not to mention all the car chases, burglaries, meetings, emergencies, and the endless cycle of paperwork. It was a thankless, pressure-filled, and unpredictable job.

He looked forward, however, to spending the rest of his life with his beloved Mabel, traveling the country. God knows he has neglected her over the years.

"God knows," coughs Mac from too many cigarettes, yet takes another drag from the one hanging on his bottom lip.

AT THE EDGE OF TOWN, in a small but dimly lit room, Ty Walker sat alone with his Bible, curled up in his favorite recliner. No words could describe this quiet display of a man with his Creator, a special time each morning when the wife and kids were still slumbering. He could concentrate better for some reason in the early hours before dawn. Ty had heard others in the church complain that it was difficult for them to study in the wee hours of the morning because of sleepiness, but no matter; this was his time.

He had been studying 1 Kings when his eye scans across the passage found in Chapter 19, reciting it quietly:

> **"... but the Lord was not in the wind. After the wind, there was an earthquake, but the Lord was not in the earthquake. After the earthquake came a fire, but the Lord was not in the fire. And after the fire came a gentle whisper. When Elijah heard it..."**
>
> **— 1 KINGS 19:11-13**

His eyes stop and stare at the last line intensely. He got lost in the wording and was engrossed by its meaning. *"Elijah heard it. Elijah heard it."* Over and over, the thought flits through his mind, deciphering, contemplating, and pondering. Leaning forward and seizing his pen, he scribbles notes about the subject on a pad that contains pages of information he had gleaned over the years. *Better write this down,* he thought. *If God spoke—and I know He did—it has the obvious reasoning that Elijah heard something. Did Elijah hear an audible voice? Was this a speaking to the mind or an impression on the soul? What did Elijah hear? This has always been the question of man throughout the centuries. How does God, our Creator, speak to us? And in what ways? How can I find the answers in the Word of God? How do we know when it is God speaking and not the Devil tricking us with our own wishes or ideas?*

He pauses briefly, wincing at the last statement. It was this point where he ascertained that many had gone astray from their own imaginations or "notions of the flesh" as Ty calls them. He had seen variations of them through the years after becoming a Christian. There were those who claimed it was the "voice and will of God" that women should not wear makeup, pants, or jewelry, or else their eternal souls were in danger. And men, not to leave them out, must be dressed in a suit and tie.

Ty began pondering how ironic this was, because during the turn of the 20th century, it was considered a sin for a man to be wearing a tie, and now it was considered rude not to. One belief that he once held (like a Pharisee) was that Christian rock and roll style music wasn't holy or Godly, until a contemporary concert in Nashville changed his perspective. There, he witnessed hundreds of youth encountering Christ—young people the traditional church had never reached and likely never would.

He had also witnessed disputes over water baptism, baptism of the Spirit, and the timing and method of baptism; each one declaring, "Thus says the Lord," yet shaped by the wishes of man in that moment. *No wonder* the *non-believers of the world are not responding. The church is so confused with the voice of God; the world sees it and does not know whom to believe.*

Ty puts down his pen, leans back in his chair, and continues rocking slowly. Closing his eyes, he begins to pray for the voice of God to be clear in every area and decision of his life.

He prays for his family, his soon-to-be child, and for the salvation of Laurie's uncle, who was an alcoholic. His prayer also concentrated on the school, the students, the staff, and especially Nettie. Just as he was about to wrap up with his prayers, he suddenly felt that familiar, nagging feeling in his chest again.

The first time Ty had felt this sensation was at a church picnic, and it stunned him. Next, was at a school board meeting, and another time was when he was talking to Charles Dunlap, Chief Engineer of Massey Dam. Also, anytime he went near Oliver Huber, Massey Lake's fish camp owner, a deep inner tug-of-war took place. Over the years, the sensations grew more frequent and stronger. They were not painful in any manner—just unpredictable. Ty had gone to Doc Waters for a complete physical check-up with an Electrocardiogram test, and he had checked out in perfect health, so he knew it was not his heart. He changed his diet, and nothing changed for the better. He ceased drinking any caffeine for a period to see if any changes took place. Nothing. He exercised by walking regularly, but the inner tugs refused to quiet; instead, they struck more often and with more force.

Why is this happening? Ty thinks as he wrestles with his thoughts. *Is there a reason to this? Is this, in a strange way, how God speaks to me? And if so, what is He saying, and how do I listen?*

Concentrating and deep in thought, the door to his room opens up with a slight creaky sound, startling him. It was Laurie.

"Good morning, hun... How do you feel?" he asks, reaching up to hug her gently.

"Oh, I'm better than I was last night. I didn't sleep well, and I really wish this little one would settle down and stop kicking me during the few hours of rest I manage to get. So, what are you so deep in thought about?" Laurie probes, rubbing her eyes and yawning.

"About how God speaks to people," in hopes of a discussion with her about the subject.

"That's nice. What do you want for breakfast? I am craving blueberry pancakes this morning. Would you like some, Ty?"

"Yes," Ty smiles at her. He recognizes that for the moment, Laurie's appetite takes precedence over theological matters. And she was in no mood to discuss anything but food.

"That feeling came again this morning."

"It did? I still say it is what you are eating. Sausage, or bacon?"

"Sausage. But I don't think that's the cause. It is almost pleasant in a strange sort of way."

"Pleasant would be delivering this baby soon," Laurie yawns again, rubbing her oversized belly, "but first, pancakes." She leaves the room, Ty laughing at his hunger-driven wife.

Gathering up all his study material, he places it on the shelf for the following morning. He walks over to the mirror and stares at his image for several seconds. *What is really going on inside you? Are you going nuts or something? What is it?*

As he turns to exit the room, a whisper—a very gentle voice calls, **"*Tyyyy.*"** The call startles him, and his heart begins to thump harder.

What was that? Who was that?

There was no one in the room. He could hear his wife in the kitchen humming a tune, so he knew it wasn't Laurie. Quickly and quietly, he rushes to the children's rooms. Ben was buried under a pile of blankets. Checking Audrey in her room, he finds her clutching a big gray teddy bear, sound asleep.

Who called my name? I know I heard my name... Is it God? He checks the hall, the stairs, and the closets. Nothing. His heart quickens as he races through the house, looking like a man possessed. Ty searches and finds no one.

"Laurie... did you call my name a few moments ago?" he asks, out of breath.

"No," Laurie says, casually mixing her blueberry pancake batter.

"I know I heard someone say my name," he exclaims with conviction rising in his voice.

"Maybe you just imagined that you did," Laurie responds nonchalantly.

Sitting at the kitchen table with a puzzled expression, Ty tries to sort out what he heard. Most times, he would agree with Laurie that he imagined it, or dismiss it as the wind, or a dog barking, or something like that, but this time... this time it was different.

Not only did he hear a voice, but he could discern a presence of power associated with the voice. *Oh yes, this time it was different.*

"Still pondering what you heard?" Laurie asks, becoming concerned with her husband's mood. "Maybe you need a break today. Why don't you go fishing at the lake? You like fishing there. As hard as you work at the school and the church with the board and all the chores, and me—"

"I get your drift," Ty interjects, stopping her flow of words with a big hug. "Perhaps it would do me some good to get away. I have a lot to think about."

Just then, the phone rings.

"Now who would be calling this early?" Laurie exclaims.

"Hello," she answers in a soft voice. "Pastor Stoddard? Oh yes, Ty's here in the kitchen. We were just having a chat. Hold on." She hands the phone to Ty.

"Good morning, Pastor."

"Good morning, Ty. I was wondering if I could meet with you later this evening, if it's convenient. I'd like to discuss some details concerning next week's board meeting. Could you meet me in the church office, say, seven o'clock?"

"Sure! I'm going fishing at Massey Lake today, but I'll be back in time. Also, Pastor?"

"Yes?"

"I need to discuss something with you also. It's a personal question about hearing the voice of God. Perhaps you have some good resources on the subject."

"I believe I can find an ample supply," he states, with a hearty chuckle. "I will have some ready for you. See you soon."

"See you soon, Pastor," Ty responds and then hangs up the phone.

After breakfast, Ty makes his way to the garage to retrieve his fishing gear. He puts on his favorite hat with a smile on his face at the thought of relaxing and reeling. Of all the words in the dictionary, two were Ty's favorite, and they spoke volumes:

GONE FISHING!

Chapter 6
Gone Fishing

The small boat gently rocks back and forth as a light breeze stirs across Massey Lake. Created in 1958 with the construction of Massey Dam, the lake has powered a wide region ever since. Ty finds himself at one of his favorite fishing spots, where vibrant oaks drape over the hill like a colorful tapestry, shedding leaves every so often. He casts his line repeatedly, skillfully working along the deep bank like a pro on a fishing show. Although luck isn't on his side today—with it being the middle of the day and the cool temperatures—he knows that bass prefer warmer weather, especially around May when they're bedding. Still, he reminds himself that bass can be caught, but only in deeper waters and with a fair bit of patience. Despite the challenges, Ty enjoys imagining himself being critiqued by a sports commentator, just like on TV. Pulling down his gray hat for a more serious look, he begins to daydream and narrate his "show":

Here we are ladies and gentlemen at the Massey Bass Classic. Ten thousand dollars rest in the coffers of prize money for the trophy bass. We'll have fair, but cool skies and a west wind. And on the circuit, newcomer Tyrel Walker will challenge many old-timers for the prize. Ty has—

Wham! A strike snaps Ty back into reality. As he sets the hook, the rod bends strongly over, and his drag on the reel begins to whine loudly. Guiding the fish toward the front of the boat, he keeps the taunt line from rubbing the edge so it doesn't snap. The fish thrashes and wiggles, trying to free itself, but soon tires out. Ty reaches down and grabs the kicking catch with his net. He estimates that it weighs around four pounds as he inspects the bass, holding it up by the mouth for his imaginary photo op before releasing it back into the water for another day.

Ty lays down his rod, grabs a sandwich, and eases back into the seat that creaks from age and neglect.

It was nice to relax and let the world go on with its rat race. And rat race it is. How things have changed in the years of teaching high school science, serving for four years as an assistant principal at Fork Mountain High School, and now the fifth year as principal of Hidden Creek. It's a different world with greater and compounding circumstances.

The students, especially. Ty considers as he rubbed his forehead. *Students are changing in exponential ways. Lack of respect, resentment of authority, disobedience to parents, fierce and angry, and seeking pleasures are just a few to mention. Sounds like the last days mentioned in 2 Timothy 3... No wonder so many people think these are the last days.*

It appears to only be getting worse with all the pressures children face with absent parents and broken homes. Experimentation with drugs, sex, and fads of the day, video games adults shouldn't even play, computers and television pushing better, faster, and more, more, more. And school systems spend millions researching why there are so many attention problems.

The issue of God is at the heart of the student's problems. Many years before, there was a movement that touted that "God was Dead." Well, in the public school system, He was. God was forced out, pushed aside, and made to be secondary to the hoax of evolution. That and the Big Bang theory; a curse from the Devil. Ty chuckles to himself, *O, I remember the time I drew a reprimand for telling my Science students about the Big Bang theory. I told them in the beginning, God said Bang! And there was a Big Bang! With no God in school, there was little room for error at home and church. Without Godly guidance from parents, pastors, and friends, these young minds were faced with enormous odds and headed for certain failure.*

Certain failure... Ty continues... *as if I had room to talk. Raised in a non-Christian home and parents consumed with making and having more, I, too, struggled in life and school. God was for the weak-minded, so I thought... not for me. Oh, I attended a few times, but it was meaningless. Making money was not meaningless; in fact, it was my "God," and I had taken up where my parents left off. Without God in my life, temptation took over, and then came THE MISTAKE.*

Ty jumped as if he had been startled from a nightmare. *Yes, THE MISTAKE. The one that changed everything.*

He could still feel the cold, dense air of the jail cell. Day after day, week after week, he grew miserable beyond words. He was twenty, arrogant, angry, and frustrated.

But during that time, an angel of mercy came in the form of an aging gentleman named John Patrick. His ministry was to meet with inmates once a week, and he took the time to explain the Gospel of God's Word to Ty.

John showed him that even mistakes could be forgiven and that God wanted to direct a man's life. One night, while they were talking, Ty had listened intently. The words were reaching him—he could feel it. A great desire within his soul leaped out to Jesus

Christ, and in that moment, he found the peace he had been searching for.

From that day forward, his life changed. Everything changed.

MOE TURNS page after page of his old, tattered Bible; his weathered hands shaking from the cool air in the room. The fire in the stove had burned out, but he paid it no mind. There was something far greater happening. Moe stops at a familiar passage. His eyes scan back and forth; his breath escapes him. Tears stream down his cheeks and across his graying whiskers.

"Pray Moe... pray!" whispers the Holy Spirit.

SURVEYING the bottom of the boat, Ty notices the patchwork showing the scars of repair, and he contemplates... *I wonder how many times Mr. Huber has repaired these old rental boats over the years.*

Oliver Wendell Huber owned the boat rental camp and launch on the west side of Massey Lake. A flavorful man in his late eighties with hardly a tooth to be seen, Mr. Huber was a businessman by trade, but a storyteller by nature. He could spin stories that people found very hard to believe, and it was impossible to be in his company for long without being treated to one of his stories, whether you wanted to hear it or not. He had various kinds of tales to tell, ranging from war stories to marriage stories; however, fishing stories were his absolute favorite. The humorous side was the fact that Oliver believed his own stretches of truth with conviction, partly because he had told them so many times over the years. Despite the fact that he hadn't visited Hidden Creek in decades, everyone adored him. He was an icon, a part of the community that would be at a loss without him.

Ty laughs to himself, thinking about the story Mr. Huber had told him countless times about Massey Lake's only flying fish—a ten-pound bass that mistook a fishing lure and Oliver's shiny bald head. Mr. Huber had insisted that the sun's reflection from his scalp drove the bass to jump out of the water toward his head. "Luckily," he would boast, "I netted the bass in midair before it could bite my ears off."

Eating as he drifts, Ty takes a deep, relaxing breath as he soaks in the astounding beauty around him. Trees of incredible colors line the banks and slopes that surround the lake. Jutting from the inclines sit boulders glistening in the noonday sun. To the south of Massey Dam, he spots a small, ragged shack about three-quarters up the hillside.

Probably deserted. I heard that an old hermit once lived there. Most of the townspeople thought he was crazy. Even Oliver Huber thought so. Now that's really a stretch.

As Ty floats along, he senses God's peace... His perfect peace... A peace that could not be described. In the midst of the moment, Ty raises both hands toward the sky and thanks God for all that He has done: for his salvation, his marriage, his children, his job, and the truly beautiful day that God has given him. During his thanksgiving, a slight twinge begins to grow in his chest.

There it is again! It feels different this time. What is happening to my body?

From the small area of his chest, an explosion was taking place, and an incredible warmth began to spread to his arms and legs, accompanied by a trembling of sorts. It was pushing and pulsing throughout his entire body.

An alarm blows off in his head... *Could it be a heart attack! If I'm having a heart attack, why does this feel so good?* His knees quiver as he kneels into the bottom of the boat, wrapped in ecstasy, in an envelope of warmth. All the clutter of life, work, and problems is vanishing. Worries disappearing. Concerns melting. Schedules evaporating. His mind is clear and focused, and the only words that could capture the experience were, simply heavenly!

Then came the voice. **"*Tyyyy.*"**

Two hours later, the boat bumped and jarred against the bank of the river, not rousing the passenger who lay prostrate on the bottom with a partially eaten sandwich still clutched in his hand. Several deer who had come to drink stood cautiously nearby, ears raised, and peering curiously at the scene, after which, they quickly withdrew to the safety of cover.

Laurie Walker stares anxiously into the growing dark, wringing her hands in silent but nervous worry. *Where is Ty? Why is he so late? He's never been this late before. I wonder if he went directly to the church office to meet the pastor.* As she reaches for the phone, it rings out, causing her to jump.

"Hello," snatching the phone and responding in a rather quick voice.

"Laurie, has Ty left yet? It's seven fifteen and I have a lot to do."

The phone almost falling from Laurie's hands with a heart pounding faster than usual, she responds.

"Pastor, Ty left this morning for Massey Lake. He was supposed to be back long ago!" Laurie's voice begins to shake, "I was hoping he was with you. Has Ty called you? He's never been this late before... I'm starting to get..." her voice trails off as she struggles to hold back her tears.

"I'm sure it is nothing to worry about," Pastor Stoddard reassures her, sensing her anxiety. "He could have had a flat coming down the mountain, or knowing Ty, he probably stopped to help someone fix a broken-down car. You know how he gets involved in others' lives. I'm certain he'll be here any minute from now."

Laurie sniffs and reaches for a box of tissues. She feels her baby now active inside her, a response to her stress. Gently, she rubs her belly, trying to find comfort.

"I guess you're right, but if Ty comes by there first, please have him call me."

"I will make it the first thing he does, Laurie," placing a large book back into his case. "I'm sure everything is going to be fine. Sometimes worry is our worst enemy."

"Just let me know, Pastor… okay?"

"Just rest. I'll have him call you the moment he arrives. I have to go. Goodbye."

"Goodbye." She hangs up the phone and looks into the eyes of her children, who were listening in on the conversation with Pastor Stoddard.

"Where's Daddy?" Audrey questions in an apprehensive, childlike voice.

"Mom, do you want me to go look for him?" asks Ben, who not only wants to play the part of a grown-up but is also getting worried about his father.

"Now, now, nobody is going anywhere. Daddy will be along soon, I promise. He just got delayed, and God knows. Yes, God knows." Her voice begins trailing in volume as she glances outside.

Meanwhile, back at the small church office, cluttered with a desk, computer, and stacks of books, Pastor Stoddard drops slowly to his knees, driven by a compulsion to pray. There's a deep sense of urgency tonight, and he feels it stirring in his spirit. Starting slowly, his prayer becomes intense, and after an hour, he finds himself lying on the office floor, exhausted. *Something is going on tonight. It has to do with Ty Walker. I know it. Lord Jesus, take care of Ty Walker... Ty, take care!*

Chapter 7
Missing

In life, there is nothing more frustrating than the unknown. Right now, Ty is several hours late. On the front porch, distraught and pregnant Laurie Walker paces back and forth, sitting between intervals, with anxiety growing in her chest.

Where could he be? Has something happened to him? What about the children? How will I support them? What am I going to do? She continues pacing as the questions race through her mind.

Once again, the baby in her tummy moves and stretches with great discomfort, making Laurie rub her belly continuously—gently, yet still with great worry. The situation was more than she could take. The most dependable man on earth was missing, and there was little she could do except call the police, of course, and even they were hesitant to do anything because the twenty-four-hour missing person request was not even close. Still, she was able to convince the police to send out a patrol car to her house. And now the police were taking their sweet time getting there.

Where are the police? They should have been here by now!

Laurie wrings her hands together until her knuckles turn white and her fingers red, as she walks outside.

Sitting on the front step, she's comforted by a warm sweater on the cool night. Laurie stares anxiously for any sign of Ty or the police.

Focusing into the space, she starts to think, *"Why, God? Why do I worry and have a fear of losing him? Why can't I trust you? Why can't I accept that Ty is in your care, and even if I should lose him physically, he still is in your care?* She shudders at the thought of that. *This is not something I ever thought I would consider. If I lose him, it would wreck my entire life.*

Deep in thought, the flash of headlights turning onto Cinnamon Lane makes Laurie jump. She strains to see who it is. It's the police. They slowly pull into the driveway as Laurie briskly walks to the driver's door. Office McMurphy steps out, grimacing slightly from his bad back and being overweight.

"Mac, where have you been? I called the station over two hours ago... Ty's missing, and seeing how you two are such good friends, I figured... Well, I figured you'd get here sooner." Her frustration was evident.

"Laurie, I tried to leave sooner, but I got tangled up filling out reports. You know how that can get. Then on the way, I had to call in an accident that took place on Carlisle Street, and of course, more forms—"

Interrupting his stream of words, Laurie blurts out, "Oh, Mac, I'm so worried. It is not like Ty to be late. And to make me worry would be unheard of!"

Mac knows very well that Ty is not inconsiderate. Since they had become friends, they hunted together every fall and winter for whitetail deer and wild turkey in the early spring. It was Ty's persistence that wrestled Mac from his couch potato habit during hunting season for fun and exercise. Not only that, but Ty also persuaded him to try the Community Church on occasion, although Mac held little stock in religious faiths. He believed in a God, but incorporating God into everyday life was different. He had seen too much crime and pain as a police officer to believe love existed in the way Ty described love. However, if real love existed, Mac had found some form of it in Ty Walker.

Mac remembers when Ty showed up after his wife Mabel broke her hip from a fall and left him with a house load of chores, not to mention his police duty. Ty had helped with cleaning, cooking, running errands, and even doing some yard work. Yes, in Mac McMurphy's mind, there was no one on earth like Tyrel Walker.

"Now Laurie..." placing his arm around her shoulders. "I'm sure he's fine. He'll be here before you know it. Where did Ty go today?"

"He left to go fishing at Massey Reservoir about nine this morning, and he was supposed to meet with Pastor Stoddard at the church at seven... which he didn't make it to either."

"Did he say if he was going to stop anywhere else or do anything else today after fishing?"

"No, Mac. He wanted to get away to relax."

"Any calls?" inquired Mac.

"No," her voice began breaking into a cry. "I wish I knew Mr. Huber's phone number. I would have already called him to see if Ty got there, and if he had, what time he had left?"

In that moment, tears start flowing down Laurie's cheeks, her body shaking intensely with each sob. The whole situation was beginning to break her mental toughness. It was she at the ladies' Bible study who gave the encouraging advice to others that "*The Lord is in control and that all things work out for those who love Him.*" Right now, her advice to others feels and looks so distant. She thought of herself as hypocritical. Laurie grabs the post of the front porch in the overwhelming moment.

"Laurie, technically, I can't file a missing person report until the twenty-four-hour period is up, but because it is Ty, I'll drive up the mountain after my shift is over to see if he's broken down. That is probably what happened," Mac said, in an effort to soothe her troubled heart.

"I'll check back with you if I locate him." Mac climbs back into the squad car, and he leans out the window. "He will show up, Laurie. Ty is not the kind of man who will keep you worrying."

"Thanks, Mac," she utters as she wipes the streams from her face. "But if he is not here by morning, I'm going to find him myself."

"Laurie, I'll find him. Don't you worry. I've been in this business for a long time. You just rest and try to calm down. You'd better get inside... the rain is headed this way by the looks of those clouds." A loud clap of thunder follows the quick flashes of light.

Rolling up the window, Officer McMurphy drives off as Laurie watches his taillights disappear into the darkness. Standing in the front yard, with anxiety knotting in her tummy, she feels a profound helplessness wash over her, with her heart racing and different thoughts traveling through her mind. She realizes that all she can do right now is wait.

Laurie feels a strong discomfort in her abdomen as the baby stretches roughly. Her hand smoothly moves over the tummy area again and again. "Now, now, don't you start worrying too. I'm doing enough of that myself for the both of us," she softly speaks.

A drop of rain and then another snap her out of deep thoughts about Ty and the baby. The wind begins to roll in from the south, and the rain becomes a torrent of extreme weather. Laurie backs up onto the front porch to escape the sudden onslaught.

Standing there on the porch watching the storm only added misery to Laurie's mood. She whispers a short prayer to the Lord. "Lord, I hope Ty is warm and dry... no, I pray he's alive, wet or dry."

Sᴜɴᴅᴀʏ ᴍᴏʀɴɪɴɢ ʙʀᴏᴋᴇ wet and dreary with the rain continuing in a slow, steady pace after the night's downpour. Laurie, now exhausted from little sleep, moved slowly around the kitchen preparing bacon and eggs for the children, who groaned when she went to their rooms to rouse them. Ben moaned through a muffled pillow that it was too early, and Audrey glanced at her window briefly before falling quickly back to sleep.

It had been a rough night for Laurie. With all the stress of Ty not coming home, the baby kicked and poked constantly, reacting as if it, too, knew something was wrong. Several times during the night, a car sloshed by the house, and each time Laurie rushed to the window only to have her hopes dashed.

It was an emotional nightmare because of the character of the person involved—the timely and punctual man of Hidden Creek. Ty was never late to work, meetings, and especially church. Ty said his father taught him the principle of being on time with the saying, "A minute late is as much as an hour late." And now Ty was nowhere to be seen, and it was seven twenty in the morning.

Laurie leans back in her chair, sipping some decaffeinated coffee; her mind is a wreck from worry and lack of sleep. Her hands are trembling as she raises the cup slowly to her mouth. *Where are you, Ty? Where are you?*

Iɴ ᴛʜᴇ ᴡᴇʟʟ-ᴋᴇᴘᴛ but old shotgun home on Dove Street, Moe Wilson lay exhausted on his couch, asleep from the long day of prayer that reached deep into the night. It had been as intense as though he were preparing for a marathon. The old, tattered Bible lay open where a passage had been circled numerous times by one who would appear possessed:

"The works of his hands are faithful and just; all his precepts are trustworthy. They are steadfast forever and ever, done in faithfulness and uprightness. He provided redemption for his people; he ordained his covenant forever - holy and awesome is his name."

— PSALM 111:7-9

STEERING the old family car up the winding road, Laurie Walker set out to begin the search for her husband.

The fog posed to be a huge problem as visibility was very limited, and slight rain was just enough to make Laurie periodically hassle with the windshield wiper switch. Around every curve, she strained with the hope of seeing the Roughrider parked on the side of the road or perhaps on a logging road cut by Miller Paper Company.

Ben was her lookout for the dirt roads cutting away from the rear of the car. He, too, anxious to find his father, jumped at the chance when he noticed an old truck and a work tractor left by the loggers. Both times, Laurie's heart skipped a beat, only to be filled with disappointment at the result.

Audrey, on the other hand, lay curled up in the backseat, sound asleep from the ride and the weather, with one of her dolls.

Glancing back at her peaceful state, Laurie wondered how this was affecting her. *Oh, how Ty adores her, and she adores him in return. I've got to find him... I just have to!*

Up ahead, the turn to Massey Dam presented a dilemma for Laurie.

Should I turn here to check at the dam or go on to Huber's launch? She sits at the intersection for a few minutes, racking her brain, trying to decide. The dam was only two miles at best, and it would only take ten minutes. *But what if...*

Twirling the steering wheel to the left. Laurie drives rapidly toward the dam from her decision.

Perhaps he broke down and coasted the car down the hill? He knows Charles Dunlap. I'd bet that is the case. But why didn't he call from the dam?

As she nears the dam, a lone vehicle cuts through the fog, gliding past Massey Dam Road and making its way down the mountain.

Meanwhile, Ben steps out of the car and rings the buzzer at the locked gate to the entrance of Massey Dam. A few moments later, a middle-aged man with peppered gray hair and a mustache peeks through a small window of the security door. His slow movements display his unconcern, as if he had all the time in the world. Finally, he meanders toward the gate, clipboard in hand, wearing a hard hat and goggles.

"Mr. Dunlap?"

"Yes, can I help you?" His gravelly voice carried over the sound of water and plant activity.

"Mr. Dunlap, I'm Ben Walker, Ty's son. My mother and I are looking for my father. Have you seen him?" he asks with a quivering voice. The misty rain had dramatically lowered the temperature.

"So, you're Ty's boy," responding with a broad smile.

"Yes, sir. Have you heard from or seen my father in the last two days?"

"No, son, sure haven't. It's been kinda quiet here lately. He's missing, huh? If I see him, you can count on me to help. He sure is a good man, your dad."

"I know, and thanks," Ben turns and runs toward the car. "Mom," says Ben as he quickly slides into the passenger's seat, "he's not here. Mr. Dunlap hasn't seen him."

Stepping on the gas a little hard, the tires squeal on the wet pavement. Laurie speeds faster even though the weather conditions are deteriorating. Getting back to the main road, she turns left to go to Huber's launch.

"Here, chick, chick, chick," squawks Oliver Huber as he scatters feed corn on the ground inside the makeshift chicken coop he built behind his house.

"Aw, Bessie," he says, talking to his favorite hen, "keeping the ol' bottom warm, I see. Heh, heh, just keep laying them vittles, and ya won't hear nothin' from me."

Looking around, he sees Dynamite, a strutting and dominant rooster who's charging the others for food. "Now, Dynamite, back off ya hungry rascal! Give me hens some feedin' room," shooing the colorful cock back so the others could eat.

The sound of crackling gravel at high speed on the road leading up to his launch drew Oliver's attention. He scattered the rest of the feed, dropped the bucket, and walked around the side of the coup just as Laurie and her children arrived. Oliver stood curiously with his hands in his overalls. His snowy eyebrows narrowed, indicating his wariness of the strangers who slid to a stop in the half-gravel, half-dirt drive.

"Mr. Huber?" Laurie calls as she launches from the car, causing Oliver to take a few steps back in recoil.

"Yep!"

"Mr. Huber, I'm Laurie Walker, Ty's wife," she adds, slightly out of breath from the higher altitude.

"Well, howdy do!" he grabs her hands and shakes them like she was his long-lost friend. "Sure is nice to meet you'n for the first time! Your'n hubby is a fine man... one of the best'uns! My, my, Ty told me you were on the nest and he wasn't joking!" Oliver's happy smile revealed nothing but bare gums. "Call me Oliver, please, won't ya?"

"Mr. Huber... Oliver, Ty is missing. Do you know where he might be, or have you seen him in the last two days?"

"Sure'n have. Rented him a skipper yesterday mornin.' Saw him headin' out toward his favorite spot, too. Didn't see him come in, though. Haven't checked me ol' skippers this mornin'. Foller me, and we'll find out if'n he came back."

The old man limped slowly down the slight grade to the boat launch in his raincoat; his overalls sagged and drooped in the back, telling the story of better years. Every so often, Oliver spat tobacco juice and hummed to himself. Next to telling wild stories, humming tunes was a sort of hobby for him. They left Audrey asleep in the car.

The patched boats rocked and scrubbed in their slots from the west wind blowing across the reservoir. The slight misty rain had ceased for the moment. Oliver strolled down the wooden pier built along the bank. "Fourteen... fifteen... sixteen... Yep! Got all sixteen skippers! Hey, have you folks ever heard how I got my first'un? Let me tell ya—"

"Oliver," Laurie says impatiently, "we really don't have time for what I'm sure is a fascinating story, but we must find out where my husband is. Now, we know that he came back in from fishing, and we know he was here. Did you happen to notice his black Roughrider parked here last night?"

"Don't rightly know… go to bed with the chickens, ya see." He's scratching his bald head underneath a dirty ball cap. His wrinkled head showed intense thought, and then, as if a light came on, he piped, "Come to think of it, did hear'd somebody crank up this'n mornin' while I was stokin' ol' Molly, my potbellied stove."

"Did you notice who it was?" Ben asks, jumping into the conversation.

"Couldn't see much cause of the fog. I glanced out the curtains. Seen taillights, but wait, I did notice on the bumper an orange-looking sticker."

"Mom," broke in Ben, "that's dad! I know it!"

"Ben, we don't know for sure," Laurie cautions.

"But Mom, I put a fluorescent orange parking sticker on his bumper three days ago! Dad asked me to. He said it was for the administrative conference in Knoxville next month. You know, the conference he was excited about the other day?"

Laurie instantly remembers. Things were so cloudy in her mind, and now, it was surprising she could recall anything at all. Her husband's whereabouts were foremost at present.

"Oliver, how long ago did this vehicle leave?"

"Bout an hour, I guess," spitting more juice.

Laurie grabs Ben's arm. "The dam! When we turned for the dam! We missed him! I had a feeling. I could feel his closeness to me. Ben, load up! Your father is heading home!"

Oliver Huber leaned against the graying fence, spitting and humming as he watched the Walker family wheel away in the gravel. His bony right hand waved a weak goodbye. He turned to go back to his chores, and a tune came to mind, a tune from his past, a tune from when he at one time was a very religious fellow, *"Rock of ages… cleft for me…"*

Chapter 8
Community Church

The choir, cloaked in red robes and gold sashes, sang a rousing and ambitious closing song. Its upbeat tempo had the Community congregation on their feet, clapping and stomping to the rhythm despite the rainy, sloppy weather outside. Many were swayed by the music and spirit of the moment. A youngster no more than twelve years of age rattled a tambourine and kept perfect time while some of the elders walked and others ran briskly 'round and 'round the room ("blessed"), as if they were corralling the participants inside the pew region. It was the conclusion of a moving and inspiring service with one exception—the Walker family.

Notably conspicuous was the vacant pew in the third row on the left side of the middle section. It stood out like a glaring void—a vortex of emptiness that no one dared to occupy. Being creatures of habit, each had staked a territorial pew sitting in the same place week after week. Ironically, it helped the congregation in ministry; each knew who had come and those who had not. A missing person or family immediately drew a visit, card, or call to determine their absence.

The Walker family never missed, period. Sunday after Sunday, Wednesday nights, revivals, missionary meetings, and special services, all these, and never had they failed the Lord in attendance. Not from duty, but desire, the desire to be with the Lord's people in every aspect of their lives. And now, they were missing. Not there. Gone.

Pastor Stoddard wrapped up the service with prayer, remembering those who have not been able to join them. In each of the "regular's" minds, the Walker family was top priority. It was a very odd and unnerving feeling for each of them to have one of the pillars of the church missing.

Standing at the exit in the foyer, Pastor Stoddard senses the anxiety in each member as they crowd the area, gathering hats, raincoats, and umbrellas. Collecting their belongings, quiet murmurs float throughout the room about the prominent family.

Where are they? Are they ok? What could have kept them from coming?

Pastor Stoddard, too, feels an inward urge to know their whereabouts. Still, he shakes hands and thanks the people for coming without letting them know his feelings and thoughts—Ty's absence, Laurie's call, his painful prayer time the previous night, and now the entire family missing a service. It was all extremely unusual.

Eunice Thorton, Nettie Driscoll's informant of the Community Church gab, huddling against the wall, is taking in all the comments made about anybody and anything.

She is an introverted woman by nature in her late forties, possessing a sharp mind that collects data for her late-night phone calls to her friend, Nettie. She has grown very warm with Nettie, talking late into the night about this and that. It is a secret friendship she needed since her husband left her for another woman in Sipley, forty miles east of Hidden Creek. All she has left are her cats and Nettie, who understands her, comforts her, and consoles her. Eunice knows that Nettie uses her information and latest gossip against others, but that didn't matter; Nettie provided the companionship she desired.

With primal alertness, Eunice's attention zeroes in on Gidget Mayhew, a talkative blonde who moved to Hidden Creek seven months prior. She was already well known in the short time she had been a resident in town due to her gabbiness and ability to stretch the truth to make a story sound enticing and unique. Caught up in the moment, she babbles out in front of everyone.

"I heard from Wanda, who heard from Sally, that Ty abandoned his poor wife and kids to go fishing and hasn't come home. It sure is a shame that so many men are inconsiderate to their wives. Did any of y'all know the statistics of how many men leave their families and never return? And let's not leave out the ladies either. I heard from Lula Banks that Maggie Stewart, Mr. Walker's secretary, is missing too. Drove off with nary a word. Kind of peculiar, don't y'all think... and no one has heard a peep from either. It's disgraceful, just disgraceful you know—"

Pastor Stoddard pauses his goodbyes to stop the onslaught that was about to consume the Walker family. "Now, Gidget, stop to think about what you are doing. The Scriptures tell us specifically that, the tongue is a fire. Who can tame it?' I would highly recommend that you leave the subject alone before someone gets hurt."

"But I am telling the truth. Can the truth be wrong?"

"The truth can be twisted, Gidget. That is the problem. It can be twisted to create suspicion in the minds of others that ordinarily would not exist. Would Jesus do that? I think not! I advise that you pray for the Walker family and Miss Stewart."

With that, Gidget Mayhew bows her head in remorse, her words fading beneath the weight of the pastor's logic.

"I'm trying to follow Him pastor, but too often I fail," she answers sorrowfully.

Eunice, however, holding her purse and umbrella, was not so sympathetic. Soaking the information in like a sponge without hearing the pastor's correction, she hurries out into the rain to race home. *Nettie will love this! It is just the ticket to get a long conversation started that will last and last.* Folding her umbrella up and shaking off the rain, she cranks the old but reliable Plymouth and speeds away.

"Glad you came this morning," pipes Pastor Stoddard to the last person exiting the double doors at the back of the foyer. Waving goodbye, he closes the doors and slides the ancient brass-coated lock bars in place.

Turning toward the sanctuary, he takes a deep breath sighing; his mind contemplative and tired at the same time. The distinctive tap of his shoes on the hardwood floor echoes in the now hollow room as he makes his way to the altar. Drawn to the altar was more fitting. Pulled. Magnetized. *Pray. I must pray. I have to pray.*

His knees thump the floor with a hard thud as his body collapses upon the altar. Soon the pastor's petitions and tears run together as he begins to slide off the altar and lie on the floor. He ignores the howling weather outside; ignores the fact that dinner waits; ignores everything except reaching God about what is going on.

After a few hours, he gathers himself, locks the back door, and goes home to eat a cold dinner.

～

"Momma, it's ok. We'll find him," comforts Ben.

Laurie sobs uncontrollably with her face in her hands. Ty is nowhere to be found. She had expected to see his truck parked in the yard when they arrived, only to have her hopes dashed once more. Racing then to the church and finding everyone gone adds misery to the already depressing moment.

Now, back at home, Laurie breaks down and trembles in fear and sadness. "Where is your father?" she whimpers between sobs to Ben.

"I... I... don't know," he says, hanging his head and wondering what to do.

"Two children and one on the way!" she cries, grabbing her kicking womb.

"What am I going to do if... something has happened to your father? I can't support us all. What can I do? What..." Her words were drowned in tears and sobs.

"We can trust God, can't we?" asks Ben in timid response.

"I can't trust anything right now!" she snaps at her son and then freezes, realizing that she should not have spoken that way. "I'm sorry, Ben. I'm so sorry!" She reaches over and hugs him tightly. Audrey stares with tearful eyes at the scene, while hugging her soft teddy bear.

"Nettie, this is Eunice. I know it's early for me to be calling, but I have got some news for you that you will not believe!" Her hands and voice wavered from the incredible excitement she felt pulsing through her body.

"Now what has got you so stirred up in the middle of the day?" inquires Nettie, somewhat uninterested as she reaches for a chocolate-covered cherry and bites into the side of it.

"Some info that will change everything... especially your work. It will change your position." Eunice dangled the last three words like a carrot in front of a hungry horse, knowing that Nettie always wanted to be the "head person" at Hidden Creek High.

"What?" Nettie pleads.

Chapter 9
The Daily

A press in the rear of the *Hidden Creek Daily (The Daily)* whirls and clanks, spitting out the news prepped for the day. Ron Williams, press operator—covered in multicolor inks—sits close by drinking strong, hot coffee long before sunrise. Several stacks of the Monday edition are ready on racks, awaiting delivery personnel to pick up at 10:00 a.m. Around the press lies a pile of trash from setup runs that were not of high quality. Ink stains colored not only the floor but several lower blocks of the wall from years of being in business. Above the press hangs a large motto sign that reads:

HIDDEN CREEK DAILY NEWS
Where Nothing is Hidden

Ron leaned back and rocked in the old brown high-back chair next to the small heater the owner provided, keeping rhythm with the press. In his hands were two worn drumsticks that he tapped continuously on anything and everything that made a sound. It helped him stay awake before the rest of the employees came in at 8:00 a.m. each day.

There's my crew. He laughs to himself. *And what a crew it is!*

Richard "Rick" Rider would be the first to arrive, rushing and shoving papers all over his desk with his latest scoop as an up-and-coming news reporter. Aggressive, determined, and willing to scrape the bottom of the barrel for any story or any dirt on anyone described the dubious character of Rick Rider. In fact, Rick took the company motto to extremes. There were no limits, no holds barred, no reputation too sacred to report and tear down. He felt it to be his "journalistic duty" formulated by a concept he had learned and incorporated from professors in his liberal journalism college.

There were drawbacks, though. Excluding Nettie Driscoll, Rick was perhaps the most disliked person in the Hidden Creek area. Ron despised him. From the onset Rick was hired, he ordered and shoved Ron around like his whipping boy, telling him to *"do this and do that" and that he was "just a printer."* Secretly, Ron hoped that soon another paper like the *National Dishonor* would put Rick on staff, and he would be rid of a lot of aggravation. Besides, Rick would be a perfect fit, and then the whole country could hate him.

Next, Becky Woodruff arrived with an armload of work she had carried home the night before (usually due to the orders from none other than Rick Rider). Becky was a pleasant, easy-going lady in her late twenties who was attractive but not married or even dating. Ron treated Becky with kindness and respect not only because she was a longtime friend, but secretly, he felt a deep love for her. The thought of taking Becky out on a date was ever-present on his mind, although he didn't have the courage to ask. With Rick Rider, asking was not a problem. Becky was his doormat on which he wiped his feet every day. Her laid-back mannerisms were too easy to conquer for Rider, and he took advantage of every weakness or crack in her character.

Shortly thereafter, Sid Brumley, Chief Editor and Owner, slid his pickup into the graveled parking lot, signaling his anticipation to get started not only with the news but with numerous cups of coffee and an endless stream of cigarettes. Sid was a gruff sort of man who rarely smiled, seldom shaved, and had a sarcastic attitude toward life. He lived in a modest cabin at the foot of the hills by himself, which was what he desired most (to be left alone in his spare time). However, when Sid entered his business, the bullish side of him came out. He expected perfection in every aspect of the news. He rarely gave compliments, but was quick to let others know when they didn't achieve what he expected. Climbing the backs of others is what gave Sid self-esteem.

The press continued to clank while Ron leaned back and tapped the drumsticks. Though the press was an antique, it continued to perform, and as long as it did, Sid would not buy another.

"Sure wish they'd get a new one," mutters Ron. "It's getting harder each morning to get the press set up for what Brumley insists on, and it's about time for another raise considering what I do for this hick-town paper." He glances at his watch. *Any time now...*

As if on cue and with perfect prediction, Rick Rider rushes in the front door and goes straight to his phone to check messages while shuffling papers. The phone beeps through several messaged calls that draw little response from him until it reaches one that gains his immediate attention.

"...Rick, Nettie here... Need to speak to you... Urgent... Meet you at our regular place at the regular time... Beep."

His eyebrows raise, and a smile of intrigue appears on his otherwise serious and arrogant face. *Nettie. Urgent. This must be out of this world. Last five leads from the "ol' big nose" was town rocking, and I'll be the first to know.* The smile grew more devious as his mind raced.

This may be the one that takes me to a higher level... The big time! And I can at last be rid of this small-town dribble. Brumley will hate to see me go. That's for sure! I'm the best thing that has come his way in a long time, and does he appreciate it? No! No one does. A true artist is never appreciated until after he is gone. No different here!

As Rick puffed in his pride, Becky came in huffing and poked her head around the corner with a smile to say good morning to Ron. Rick's voice in the background immediately broke up the intimate moment.

"Becky! Becky! Did you get the information for the Ken Iman story? I need those records from the city courthouse by ten! I need to know if he had any priors. We cannot publish unless we have all the facts."

"I will try to get it for you this morning, first thing." She only said that to defuse him.

"I needed it yesterday. Don't you understand? It is news! News!"

"I am sorry, Rick. I promise to try harder."

"By the way, have you started to make some coffee yet?" he barks. "You know how that reject of a press operator loves to empty the pot before I get here!" Rider made sure he said it loud enough to goad Ron, and he succeeded in his quest.

Up and out of his seat in a flash, Ron looks around the corner at Rick and speaks with seething conviction, "Fix your own this time, Hot Shot!" Ron knew he would probably get a lesson for his outburst from Brumley later that morning about how to get along with other employees or something along those lines.

"Are you talking to me, little man?" says Rick with a face of interrogation and arrogance.

"I think you heard me! Do I have to say it twice unless you're a little slow in the head, which is possible? I believe it is time you learn how!" Turning towards Becky, Ron takes the pot and asks, "Would you like the last cup before Rick here makes us a new pot?"

Becky smiles and extends her hand, holding her "Life is Great" cup.

"Why... you little ink blot! Do you really think that Rick Rider would stoop and lower himself to a level such as yours? I am the one who really makes this paper work. I am the one who really makes the bacon, so this rag can stay open. I am—"

"Yeah, you am," Ron chimes in, "but with a "h" in front of the am!" Becky giggled loudly.

The situation grows tense as the two start toward each other, but before the shoving match begins, Sid Brumley's truck slides into the graveled drive, and he enters in typical form—grumpy, unshaven, and ready to work.

"Good morning, Sid," Becky says cheerfully as she does every day.

"Tell me what's so good about it," he mutters while hanging up his coat. "Ron, are those copies ready? Pickups are going to be 9:30 a.m. from now on. Customers are complaining! Get a move on!"

Rick sneers in glee at Ron getting chewed on, but before he could get back to the shelter of his own office, Brumley blasts out his name.

"Rider! Get in here! Where is the copy for tomorrow? I thought I told you I want to always be one day ahead! Do I need to get a new reporter who will do what I request?"

"Well, no..." replied Rick sheepishly.

"Then where is my copy?"

"Uh... I'm working on it."

"If I don't have a copy on my desk in two hours, you'll be working on it—finding a new job! And where are the great stories you keep telling me you can dig up? All you have been giving me lately is meaningless dribble! I want substance! Substance! Do you need a dictionary to discover what that means?" Brumley continues to huff in frustration, as he shuffles papers back and forth while Rick slithers in shame back to his office.

"Rider!" Rick jumped. "Get back in here and bring some coffee with you on the way!"

"It's empty."

"Well, make some then," he growls. "You have got a mind and two hands, don't you? Or are you so incompetent that you cannot even make coffee? And you call yourself a newsman! Ha!"

Becky laughs quietly as she watched the great Rick Rider fetch water to make coffee. Then, Ron breaks out into a quiet song of "Happy Days Are Here Again," with the clanking of the press.

Chapter 10
Nettie Driscoll

Steering her old Ford underneath a large oak tree at the edge of town, Nettie Driscoll turns off her lights, takes out a stick of gum, and tunes into her favorite station while she waits. The night looks clear after the storm the previous day, and the three-quarter moon gives the place a romantic glow. This is her special meeting place with Rick, where they share local gossip and possibly find companionship, something she's longed for with him.

Ten more minutes, she mutters, glancing at her watch. She checks her hair and makeup quickly, for the third time. *Impressions are everything in this world, and I sure want to impress you, Mr. Rick Rider!*

Although Rick was a younger man, Nettie felt confident that they were meant for each other, although he did not realize it yet. And she was out to help him find that out, even if it killed her. The passing of time had been the real culprit for Nettie. Aging was taking away the natural beauty she possessed in her younger years, and it was bothering her greatly. She had not been whistled at in years. However, Rick appeared, and things seemed to be getting better.

Nettie's feelings toward Rick evolved slowly. Initially, the focus was solely on local news. Now, months later, all motives had become attraction. She could see the look in his eyes toward her—it was attraction! She was also certain Rick was headed for greatness, maybe a network news anchor or a syndicated journalist, or even an important government position. Whatever. Wherever. She intended to be and go with him. Love, companionship, fulfillment, it was all going to be met in Mr. Rick Rider!

"Come on... I want to see you..." she whispers in a husky voice.

Rick Rider is in no hurry. Before leaving his apartment, he reads his mail while sipping on a glass of good, quality bourbon. He walks to the mirror and combs his hair several times, admiring how great he looks. Confidence reeks from his vain, self-absorbed look in the mirror. He knows full well that he's keeping Nettie waiting.

So what? She will wait. She'd wait all night if I let her.

He knows Nettie has fallen for him, and he intends to use the infatuation to its limit. So what if he will have to buzz her off one day? If she gives him coverage stories, he will act out her little romance novel. Smiling at his reflection in the mirror again, he mutters out loud: "To get to the top, you encounter the little bumps along the way. Nettie is one of those bumps."

A LONE MAN hoists his supplies over his back and hikes slowly up the trail of the Highland Mountain face, trying to be careful of loose rocks. His face determined, yet peaceful.

Aiming his flashlight up the trail, a glimmer catches his eye from a shiny post stuck in the ground.

"There... there it is," he whispers. He pauses for a moment, bows his head in silent prayer, then lifts his gaze skyward to investigate the starry night.

Nettie Driscoll starts growing impatient from waiting for so long. She taps her long nails on the steering column harder and harder as time passes. It was beginning to become irritating, and yet, the waiting just made her want Rick more.

He knows I'm waiting for him. Come on, won't you?

A glaring set of headlights turning onto the dirt road leading to the hideaway made Nettie jump. It must be Rick—she recognizes the car immediately. The right front running light is still out, which he never bothers to fix. As the car rolls to a stop beside hers, Rick lowers the window.

Frustrated, she leans over and pleads, "Come over and join me in the car for more privacy." Her voice is filled with the desire of wanting to be close to him.

Turning off his car, Rick meanders to the passenger door of Nettie's Ford. He notices the air is heavier with perfume tonight. *Oh no! I hope she's got some real news and hasn't dragged me out for nothing except to be with her!*

Reaching back into his actor's closet, Rick plasters on his best "good to be with you" smile, melting Nettie's heart.

"I am so glad to see you, so happy, babe. It makes me happy. You see..." She stops mid-sentence as she reaches over and runs her fingers across his neck and into his hair.

Fighting the urge to cringe, Rick interrupts her action, "Like I said earlier, what's up? His stomach tightens with discomfort, but he lets her continue for the sake of the information he seeks.

"Why are you always in a hurry, Rick? You just got here. So, relax, hun."

"I can't relax!" Rick snaps, cutting her off. "Brumley at *The Daily* is on my back about finding good stories, and if I can't supply them, he might give me the boot!"

"Brumley!" Nettie scoffs. "Always Brumley! Sid Brumley is the grouchiest, meanest, chain-smokingest, most unlikable person I have ever known! And you work for the old Scrooge! Rick, you are ten times the newsman Brumley could ever be, and one day you will see the rewards of your talent somewhere else… with me, of course."

Rick takes in an ego-boosted breath. She is working for him for sure, but deep in the recesses of his mind, he knows that Nettie is never going anywhere with him. No way!

Gathering himself back to focus, Rick presses, "What kind of news do you have for me, Nettie?"

"Ty Walker," she says, licking her lips.

"The High School Principal?" Rick narrows his eyes.

"Yep. Seems he has disappeared. Sheriff Mac is searching for him. Laurie, his expecting wife, is all upset, and the whole congregation at Community Church is buzzing about it. Missed work today, too. Bet he doesn't show up tomorrow either."

"So, a man's missing? Big deal. What is the real story?" Rick knows Nettie well enough to know that she would string along the story just to make it juicy.

"Maggie Stewart, Ty Walker's personal secretary, is gone too." Nettie smirks. "Three days ago, I caught them holding hands at school. Both said that Maggie had spilled some coffee on his coat when I knew better! Those two have had several secret little meetings, which were not so secret as you can see from the dates I have recorded," handing Rick a copy of the dates. "I have noticed the frequency has increased in the last five months. My guess is that we have two lovebirds who have flown the coop."

A frown starts to build up on Rick's face as he responds, "An affair? That's what you have? Town gossip?"

"No. That's not all. I knew you would want more!" Reaching for her purse, she takes out an envelope. "Here is what you are looking for," acting like a lawyer who delivered the death knell in a case. "Read and weep!"

Rick scans the paper slowly. His hands are trembling as his mouth drops open. He rereads the lines, making sure he understands what is being implied. If it's true, this could be the story of a lifetime.

"Are you sure about this?" Rick asked with an inquisitive reporter tone.

"I am sure as the sun will rise tomorrow, hun." She scoots closer to Rick.

"But are you absolutely, positively sure? This could land the paper and me in a serious slander suit, not to mention the possibility of shutting down the paper and the loss of my job!"

"I thought you despised *The Daily*. You are always saying you want to get away from the small-town news and move on to bigger and better places," she purrs, licking her lipstick to be more suggestive to him.

"Yeah, I know. However, that ragtag paper pays my bills. Besides, I don't want to take a load of baggage like an ugly libel suit into the office of my next employer! So, I ask you once more. Are you certain of what I hold here in my hands?"

Nettie smiled a devilish smile, "Have I ever been wrong before?"

Rick smirks, "No, my dear, not ever." He responds as he folds the paper and slips it into his coat pocket, already plotting his next move—how to deal with Brumley!

But Nettie has other plans. "And Rick, I know you can't say no to me now," she says to Rick as he tries to escape from the car.

Cupping his face in both hands, she kisses him with a passion that had been building all evening.

To Nettie, it was bliss.
To Rick, it was disgusting.

Chapter 11
Hermit Cabin

Ty Walker, covered by blankets, peered out; his face glowed in harmony with the fire and reflections. What had brought him to this position and place made no sense—except God. He had left behind so much: his wife, family, job, friends, his respect in the community and church. Everything! Nothing in his life had ever transpired like what had taken place in a matter of days. One moment fishing, the next moment, *THE VOICE*. Every step Ty took, every decision he made, every choice was guided by *the voice*. There was no doubt who *the voice* was.

Ty was told where to go, what supplies to buy, where to hide his vehicle, where to find the old trail, and where to find the cabin. Even where to find a barely visible post in the ground near the cabin containing an old key. What this all meant and where this was going, Ty had no clue, but he knew for sure that there was a purpose in all of it because of *the voice* of the Lord leading him.

He warms himself beside a makeshift fire, holding a rustic key and a dusty book, alone with the Lord.

"There it is! Take it! Absorb the contents..." speaks the voice of the Lord.

Ty examines the cover made of deer hide and the leather straps woven throughout. It was well preserved except for the heavy dusting. Wiping the layer from its face, the letters "O" and "H" appear, like the cross on the tabletop. Opening to the first page, Ty finds its owner and author:

Journal of Oren Hastings
"In the year of our Lord, which all are His anyway."

"Laurie, Sheriff Mac here," he says, shifting his weight in his office chair. "No leads yet on where Ty may be, but we have deputies and a few volunteers checking surrounding towns to see if he's been spotted buying gas, groceries, or whatever. We're also passing out fliers from the photo you gave us, posting them in the Post Offices and the like. I'm sure we'll locate him soon. No one can just vanish without leaving a trail of some kind. Are you and the family okay? Can I do anything else to help you out?"

"No," her voice trembling and beginning to break. "Just find him, Mac! That's all I want. Please, just find him!" Laurie breaks down sobbing.

"We will, I promise. It's getting late. I'd better let you go and get your rest. Thought I'd kind of keep you informed on what was going on."

"Mac," she pauses, "sleep? I haven't slept in days, and I can't! Thanks, though," she mumbles through the tears and hangs up.

Officer McMurphy leans back in his chair, rubbing his forehead from the stress, as he reaches for a cigarette.

<u>*February 20, 1939*</u>

Built this here cabin with me own hands, thanks to the Lord who gave me these hands to work with, and all the supplies of trees I could ever need. Came here after the "shiners" found out I had turned to Jesus and didn't want to make shine anymore. They figured I'd turn all of 'em in to the revenuers, so they put out a contract on my head. Had a couple of close calls in town before I got out with some grub and traps.

Quiet here and kind of lonely, but reckon to have plenty of time to pray and study those words the travelling preacher spoke about— that we all sin, and we need a Savior who can rescue us. The preacher said that Jesus came into the world to save sinners, of which I was, of course. The entire time he was preaching, something inside of me was happening. I knew that I needed Jesus in my life–Oh! What a wicked life I had lived! So much I had to be sorry for!

Before I knew what I was doing, I came forward on that homemade sawdust floor, bowed down, and asked for forgiveness! I laid it all down, and it was like a giant load rolled off my back! I was free! Really free for the first time in my life!

Through the tears and the sounds of other seekers, I felt a strong hand upon my back. Looking up, I gazed at the preacher and his eyes filled with tears of happiness for what had happened to me.

"Thank you, preacher!" I cried in a loud voice.

"Don't thank me. I didn't save you. Only Jesus can save!" he said with conviction in his voice. "I'm a man just like you–a sinner saved by the Savior."

Before we parted that glorious night, I gathered his name– Hubber... no, Huber was his name. O. W. Huber was that preacher.

AT THAT, Ty drops the journal in surprise. Huber? Oliver Wendell Huber was a preacher at one point in his life? It just can't be! Huber is a friendly sort of man, a little eccentric old-timer, but Ty had no idea about this fact of his life. Ty continues reading.

<u>April 17, 1940</u>

Surviving pretty good. Trapping is going along just fine. Made a water collection pipe below the cabin on Granite Rock to catch rainwater and snow melt-off. Been studying these Scriptures here and believe the good Lord's brought me here for a reason.

Found a mountain spring a mile east near an overhang rock. Followed the animals to find it. Ain't it strange that God's critters know where to go to get livin' water, and man fights against findin' the livin' water He freely gives?

TY CHUCKLES to himself and thinks, *The old guy nailed that piece of theology down.* He continues to read, sipping coffee, and enjoying the background of the hermit Hastings, whom Hidden Creek perceived as crazy and weird. Page after page, however, the journal displayed incredible insight into the wisdom of God that the hermit had. It was obvious that he prayed consistently. His words reflected his attitude toward prayer, and the thoughts he expressed could have only come from God, given Hastings's limited education.

He had been a moonshiner since his early childhood, working alongside his father and grandfather. He had been carrying on a family tradition until the day he received Jesus Christ as Savior. And then... everything changed! So-called friends ostracized him. Even the family turned him away, and it was at this point that Hastings decided it would be best to move up into the mountains.

December 11, 1941

Slipped quietly into town at night and found an old newspaper somebody threw away. Read that Samuel "Pappy" Driscoll passed away. He was one of them mean'uns after my head because I knew too much about the shine business. May God have mercy on his soul!

I see a war of some kind has broken out. Folks are all upset about some bombing out in the sea a few days ago. It says a lot of young men and women were killed and wounded. Will remember to pray for their families. I know prayer works... the only thing that works!

Chapter 12
Conspiracy

It has come to the attention of the Dill County Board of Education that funds are slowly disappearing from county coffers. Since the early part of last year, some $91,000 could not be accounted for. Investigations have determined no suspects or clues as to how and where the money has disappeared to. Authorities from state and local levels are pursuing every possible angle to recover funds and bring the person or persons to justice.

Several names have been listed as possible suspects, including our own Hidden Creek High School Principal, Tyrel Walker, who serves on the Dill County Committee. A source who spoke on the condition of anonymity has produced documents that warrant the investigation of Principal Walker, who at present is unreachable. Reports also show from the Mount Vernon County Register in Oak

Hill, Nebraska, some twenty years ago, that Principal Walker was charged with theft. It states that he was found guilty of stealing $30,000 in funds—although Walker maintained steadfast innocence—from the Novell Corporation, a company that produces goods such as electronic instrumentation, pumps, and regulators. Walker served three years in jail, whereby he was released one and a half years into his sentence for good behavior. Money stolen from the corporation was never recovered.

Sources also indicate that Ms. Maggie Stewart, Principal Walker's personal secretary at Hidden Creek High School, had recently received several thousand dollars from an out-of-state depositor, states an anonymous bank employee at First National Bank. Ms. Stewart, like Principal Walker, has been missing for several days. Authorities are seeking any information on their current whereabouts.

"Are you out of your mind, Rider?" Sid Brumley growls upon reading the release Rick had prepared.

"This sounds like a gossip column! What implications are you making?" Sid was fuming as he stood up from his creaky old chair.

"But Sid... it's suspicious in every way!"

"Suspicious! Have you questioned Mrs. Walker? And what is all this anonymous garbage? We could get knee deep into a libel situation with this without the facts! I've known Ty Walker for five years, and not one bad thought comes to mind! So, get all your ducks in a row before we make a move on this perception gossip."

"Sid, I have documented proof—"

"Documented anonymous junk!" spouts Sid.

Rick straightens his jacket as if he were getting uncomfortable. Uncomfortable because he knew this would be the story of the year, and it would be his ticket out of the hillbilly torture chamber to the big-time news. With that would come all the perks—money, prestige, power, and women—especially women.

"I have been to the Walkers' house to speak to his wife, but she refuses to speak to the press about her husband's past. She seemed rather testy."

"You would be testy too, Rider, if you were eight months pregnant!" Brumley snaps, drawing heavily on his cigarette.

"We need more information, and you know it, Rider! We can't run these allegations without all the facts, without all the personal responses from Walker and Stewart. And what about the Dill County Board of Education? Do they suspect Walker in all of this? And what about these sources? Are they reliable or are they some kooks seeking attention?"

"Sid, no one can locate Walker or Stewart. And yes, the Dill County Board of Education knows about Walker's past, and he is going to face stiff questioning. I've already spoken to them."

"They know about his past?" Brumley asks, shuffling through the papers.

"Yes, they reviewed him five years ago. The Tennessee Code does not explicitly prohibit a person with a felony conviction from serving as a principal of a high school. The Tennessee Department of Education has a process for reviewing the eligibility of individuals with criminal convictions to obtain educator licensure. Therefore, it is possible that a person with a felony conviction could serve as a principal of a high school in Tennessee if they have obtained the necessary licensure and meet other qualifications. However, it is important to note that the hiring decision would ultimately be made by the school district or private school, and they may have their own policies regarding the employment of individuals with criminal records."

"Look at you, Rider, you can be a decent reporter and gather facts!" Brumley said with an insulting voice and smirking face. "So, what about these sources?"

"You don't have to worry about my source. My source is rock solid, never wrong, and I retain the right to keep them anonymous."

"Rider, this is still all speculation," interrupts Brumley.

"But Sid, we have enough alleged information to run with. I have seen you print with even less than this and not even bat an eye. Why are you so off limits with this Walker fellow anyway?"

"Walker is a good man," Sid answers gently.

"I don't want to be responsible for tearing down the character of a decent citizen."

However, what Sid kept hidden from Rider was the guilty pangs of regret over the years of stories he had allowed to run. Even more pressing was the recent discovery that he was battling lung cancer, and things didn't look good.

Sensing that his position was going nowhere, Rick reached down into his deceitful bag of tricks and pulled the string he knew Sid would respond to.

"Sid... I heard tell that Tom Waller in Sipley is going to run the story tomorrow."

"What!" Sid coughed loudly. "That rag of a newsman!"

Jackpot! Rick thought. *He has taken the bait. Now to set the hook...*

"He sure is, and he thinks he can take the county cup for the best news story of the year with it."

Rick inwardly smiled as he watched the pressure build on Sid's face. An eruption was about to take place. The well-known grudge between the two had been growing for several years and never lacked intensity or emotion.

"Waller couldn't print his own name if he tried!" Sid lurches, and his chair crashes into the wall behind him. Adrenaline was beginning to erupt.

"To even claim that what he does is news is an outrage! All he knows how to do is order people around and play the axe man!" His voice rises in pitch from his seething anger.

There, at its bare root, lies the problem. Twenty years had passed since Tom Waller fired a seasoned reporter from his staff. That reporter was none other than Sid Brumley, now owner of *Hidden Creek Daily News*. Brumley's long-time enemy was now his greatest competitor.

Looking determined, Sid snatches the release from Rick, and with his jaw set, he walks to the board and pins the story for copy. He turns to Rick and blurts, "We'll see who'll have the best story! Rider, it's running today! Call Ron! Have him here at 4:00 a.m. No! Make it 3:00 a.m.! Organize the routers to meet in my office at 7:30 a.m sharp! I may even make some deliveries myself!

Seething with anger, with his fists clenched, Sid bursts out. "Waller... newsman... We'll just see!" Exhausted, he plops into his chair, breathing heavily.

"Rider! Why are you standing around? Get going!"

Rick Rider walks out, gloating in his conquest. *This is why I'm the best,* he thought without conviction.

Chapter 13
Trio

Bacon sizzled in the cast-iron skillet, seated on the cooking grate that Orren Hastings had built into the fireplace. The smell filled the cabin along with the aroma of fresh coffee. Ty cut a slice of bread from the loaf and poured honey onto its soft, white texture.

Fresh out of locust. He chuckles to himself while eating and thinking of the scripture about John the Baptist, who lived in the wilderness eating locusts and wild honey.

What a man he must have been! People today would have called him a crazy, healthy food nut with bad breath. And what a fashionable dresser (camel skin with a belt)! But his message to society was the point: the Messiah was coming, and they needed repentance!

After getting a good night's sleep and a quick meal, he washes and shaves several days of old stubble. Shortly after, he grabs the hermit's axe and gathers sufficient wood for several days. His hands burned slightly from the task, having done little but pencil pushing for the last five years, along with endless meetings and dealing with parents.

Parents! No wonder the young people were such a mess. No discipline, respect, or quality time spent. It was as if their parents left them on the side of the road to fend for themselves, and it showed!

Even though his hands and arms ached from chopping wood, it still felt good to work. Not only that, but it gave Ty time to pray for his family. *My family. What must they be thinking?*

It was more than he could take at times, but being here was best for them, in fact, for everyone! He had to stay focused.

Focus, Ty! Focus!

Ty reaches for the journal again and begins to read where he had left off:

September 7, 1952

Oliver Huber came to visit. Somehow, he found out where I was staying, and in a way, I was glad he did. It was refreshing to see someone to just talk to. Huber also brought along a young negro man named Morris Wilson. We called him "Moe." He was a right pleasant young man with a remarkably strong faith. The stories of his life made me shake my head. He told of how his father and mother were both lynched during earlier days of Hidden Creek—how they had gotten too close to a shiner's hooch house while picking wild berries. Moe was passed from family to family until he became a drifter, and at this time, he was staying with Oliver and his wife, Ann. Oliver was "discipling" Moe, as he called it. Looked more like "disciplining" to me because Oliver made Moe walk the right line. Maybe they are the same thing.

Ty let out a chuckle. *Another nugget of truth for the old guy who lived a hermit's life. Hastings was full of nuggets, and they were not gold, but spiritual truths,* he mused.

<u>January 22, 1953</u>

Our trio of fellowship of Oliver, Moe, and I have become something special. We are more than just friends. We are friends who love the Lord, pray, and study the Scriptures together. Aw... we argue every once in a while about what the good book says, but it's all in good fun. Oliver is ornery as ever about his view or his "terpitation," as he calls it. I know he means well, but he wears on the brain. Moe and I think we know why. We believe Oliver is having a difficult time. He leaves occasionally to go check on his wife, and we know she is not doing physically well. Seems she has been coughing a lot lately and has some dark spots on the inside of her arms. Oliver has a sad look about him. We have been praying for Ann for a few months now.

Speaking of prayer, Moe is growing day by day in the Lord, and he can pray like no human I have ever known. His prayers are intense and reach Heaven. I know because he gives updates all the time about answered prayers. One prayer sticks out that was not answered yet. Moe continuously says it will be answered one day! Every time he talks about it, his hands go out of control in excitement. He starts jumping up and down; his eyes get big, and his voice becomes lower, but with more power. Like what I imagine Moses sounded like when he came off the mountain after meeting with God. That prayer...

It was a typical night, I believe, in November when we gathered round the fire, told jokes, poked fun, read the good book, but that night's prayer time was different. We sat in a circle on our stump chairs, grasped hands as we always did, and began to pray. It started with personal requests and the likes, but this night, we focused more on the town of Hidden Creek. After about an hour, the room was as warm as a furnace, and I felt the love of my Savior Jesus and the love of my friends gathered with me. There were no words that I could use except HEAVENLY... This must be what Heaven will be like.

At that, Ty begins to tremble from what he, too, felt in the moment —a surge of the presence of the Lord! *This is why the Lord has brought me here! This diary! This prayer!* Again, Ty shifts his focus back onto the writings.

Moe began praying for Hidden Creek, and it was intense! I happened to look up and see beads of sweat running down his face. He prayed for the town's salvation, for the salvation of every person no matter how evil they were, and he began to mention names of families one by one, prominent to the poor. He prayed for their children and their children's children, and for anyone who would enter the city limits in the future. The room was abuzz with the presence and power of the Lord!

Oliver was shouting, "Well, Glory!" I felt that I couldn't move or even want to! Moe prayed harder and his face lifted toward Heaven! He paused. Out of his mouth came mercy cries for the moonshiners' families who had strung his parents up and all the strange disappearances of town folks.

And then... then... THEN IT HAPPENED!

THE PHONE BEGAN RINGING about one o'clock. And it didn't stop. One call after another invaded the Walker home. Neighbors, friends, co-workers, and especially church members barraged the phone line with numerous questions about Ty, his past, and his whereabouts. The story in *The Daily* had lit up a firestorm in the town of Hidden Creek. And now, the town had to know—actually demanded—the what, where, how, and why.

Many of the locals drew conclusions that Walker was guilty without a doubt, even with what little evidence they heard. Several parents screamed for him to be terminated as principal the moment he returned.

"We can't expose our children to someone like that!"

Derogatory gossip about Walker and Maggie Stewart having an affair ran rampant through ladies' groups and in the local shops. At the same time, the men held their own in tearing down his reputation by calling him a liar and a thief.

"I heard they left in the middle of the night."

The whispering around town was like a knife stabbing the heart of Hidden Creek with confusion, hurt, and distrust. More people than usual took their evening strolls by the Walker house, and several cars drove by and gawked at any tidbit they could see.

"Look at how he left her with all them kids!
They'll probably be mooching off us taxpayers soon!"

Inside, Laurie Walker was a nervous wreck. With Ben in school and Audrey at a friend's, she was alone, except for the baby kicking inside her more frequently from all the stress. Periodically, while not answering every call, she would glance out the window only to catch someone leering toward her. The Walkers were a sideshow. Once, a carload of ruffians stopped in front of their home, got out of their cars, and yelled profanities while throwing eggs at their home. They finally sped away laughing and jeering.

About the only good thing that occurred during the day was the appearance of Pastor Stoddard and his wife, Mary. They came by for a spell to check on her. Both were very comforting and compassionate toward her and tried to persuade her that there must be an explanation and reason why God was allowing this to happen. They hugged and prayed that God would give her strength.

After that, the couple mustered up their own strength to help Laurie with some overdue chores. Mary washed a load of clothes, and Pastor Stoddard repaired a leaky faucet. Laurie was thankful and collapsed into a recliner, but still felt like her world was falling apart. She was not sure of anything. One thing was for sure, however, Hidden Creek was tumbling into chaos, and the Devil himself was smiling.

Chapter 14
Moe

Rain, almost resembling snow, fell sporadically during the evening as the remaining light gave way to darkness. Being windy and cool, most animals hunkered down for the night to wait out the passing weather. A few scampering squirrels near the cabin, however, scratched and clawed for whatever they could find before retiring. Their beady eyes suddenly grew wide, ears alert, and a sharp squeal-like sound from their frightened throats sent them racing away as a large and looming stranger approached.

Inside, Ty continues reading after eating lunch and taking a long nap.

Moe was praying as no human could. The words rolled from his lips as a man possessed. He shook and quivered as a man with a fever, only this fever was the fire of the Holy Ghost! I could tell. But the words. The words. Words of meaning, encouragement, and a promise—

Tap. Tap, tap. Tap, tap…

Ty jumped suddenly! *Someone's at the door! But how? Impossible! Perhaps it was hail or large sleet or an animal scratching? No one knows where I am!*

Tap! Tap! Tap!… The sound resounded loudly through the cabin!

Easing the door open, Ty stares into the hooded eyes of an old man. His topcoat drenched from the bad weather and at his side a large duffel bag lay on the ground.

"Mr. Walker."

"Moe Wilson?" Ty stated in a confused tone.

Both stand there looking at each other in silence. Neither knew what to do next. Finally, without a word, Ty ushers the elderly man inside the cabin, takes his coat, shakes it, and hangs it near the fire to dry. Moe pulls the duffel bag to the nearest wall and lets go of it like a burden.

"Not sa' young as I use to be," shaking his gray head.

"Moe, what are you doing here, and how did you get here?" Ty probes, knowing one part of the answer before even asking the questions, but needs him to say it anyway. He had reckoned that Moe Wilson, Oliver Huber, the assumed deceased Orren Hastings, and himself were part of a plan God started in motion long ago.

"Mr. Walker, I'm here to help you… to be your servant. You are to pray. I am to serve. Got here in an old pickup that I've had for many years in a barn and haven't driven much. No need to drive, but I always kept my license up to date. I had to lay hands on and pray for the truck to start. The Lord is faithful," Moe responded, all smiles.

The frankness surprised Ty, but he marveled at his to-the-point attitude. As principal, he had spoken briefly to Moe in passing, saying hello or good morning, yet it suddenly occurred to him that this was a man he had failed miserably at getting to know.

Looking at Moe, he notices his weathered hands and face, the worn boots, and his twinkling eyes. *His eyes! The eye is the lamp of the soul,* Ty thought to himself. *This is a man of God in the truest sense.*

The fire popped and crackled, breaking the long silence. Moe stood and stoked the fire with a long iron poker, causing the fire to pop even louder.

"Mr. Walker."

"Call me Ty." Ty interrupts him almost immediately.

"Mr. Wal-uh... Ty, many ah years passed in this here very room... a wonderful thing took place. So wonderful I's don't know how to explain it. A promise came, a very special promise. Your'n part of it, and now, so am I. You are to pray, sir. I am to serve."

"What promise, Moe?" Ty's mind is racing and trying to piece together the puzzle that still lacks several pieces. "What promise, Moe?"

"You hold the answer there in your'n hands, sir. 'Tis all as Mr. Hastings wrote it, and as God intended it. I's been waiting a long time for this to be answered. The Good Lawd's faithful, not slow in His ways."

"So, it's an answer to prayer?" Ty asks quizzingly.

"Not really a prayer, sir, but a prophecy." The old man's eyes glowed with the Spirit.

"A prophecy to be fulfilled. Why it came through me, I's don't know, but the Lawd knows—His'n ways are not our'n ways. To this day, I believe it came because I truly forgave them white folks who hung my parents. I's had so much hate in my heart. 'Twas awful! I's trusted nobody because I thought everyone was like Pappy Driscoll and that bunch."

"Samuel Pappy Driscoll, the same as in the journal?" Asks Ty with an inquiring tone. "The Driscoll's hung your family?"

"Yep! And I's had it in bad for them folks. Planned on getting them back by the very few pieces of dynamite I had stolen...'till Oliver came along."

"Oliver Wendell Huber?"

"Yes, sir, the very same," nodding in affirmation. "He came into town ridin' a fine horse, a mighty fine horse, preachin', testifyin', and the like. Said no matter what we'd done, we could be forgiven by the power of the blood! A preacher like no other was Mr. Huber! He'd spit fire and brimstone outta one corner of his'n mouth, while pouring love and mercy outta the other side at the same time. When he preached, the first five rows would have thought they'd gone through the fiery pit... only, he'd put out the fire with the love of the Lawd Jesus! But it came at a price; a number of moonshiners didn't cotton to his preachin' about coming clean and repentin' over sin, so they busted him up really bad. Broke his'n leg, nose, and some ribs."

That's probably why Oliver had the limp... Ty reasoned.

"So, what happened? Why is Oliver operating a boat rental business and not preaching the gospel of Jesus today?"

"Ann," Moe said softly, lowering his head, his eyes tearing up.

"Ann, his wife?"

"Yes, sir. Seems she got sick—the spots, we called it—and died. Found out later it was tuberculosis. Mr. Huber was fond of Miss Ann, and when she passed, he kind of went crazy in grief and blamed God for takin' her. She was one fine lady; kind, warm, always helpin.' I's even miss her." The tears rolled down his weathered cheeks.

Ty pauses and lets the moment sink in, not saying anything, for he could feel the sorrow in Moe's voice about the death of Ann Huber and Oliver's grief. He was discovering the history of Hidden Creek piece by piece.

"Moe, you called the promise a prophecy," Ty says while getting back to the original subject. "What did the prophecy say?"

Wagging his finger back and forth as if to imply he would not answer, and eyes widening with a gleam, Moe finally points toward the journal. In an almost mystical voice, he whispers, "In there, sir, in there..."

Chapter 15
Prophecy

"**N**ettie. Rick here." Rick was excited and breathing heavily. "We've hit the big-time girl!" He quickly glances around from the gas station phone booth to see if he is being watched.

"The story is incredible, and I owe it all to your info! It has taken the town by storm. Brumley is beside himself with all the attention, the phone calls, and the brouhaha from the reporters out of town. The phone has rung off the hook, and Ronny boy is having to work a double shift to print not only for Hidden Creek, but for nearby towns who are greedy and lusting for the news! It's as if God Himself—if there is one—has sent all of us a present from above!" he exclaimed, coughing as he mentioned '*God.*' He despised Christians and their goody-two-shoe ways.

THE PHONE RANG REPEATEDLY at the Walker residence, and Laurie picked it up each time, hoping it would be Ty, but as time went along, she realized with growing frustration how truly awful people can be. The calls were getting uglier and viler by the minute. With the news about her husband circling ever wider, she had to focus even through the tears and sorrow of each call not being from her husband. The phone's tune startled her out of her thoughts again, making her jump.

"Hello," she says in a frustrated tone, bracing for expected garbage talk.

"Laurie?" responded Maggie Stewart, reacting to the tone of the woman she knew as a friend, and certainly not one to be rude at any cause. "Laurie, is that you?"

"Maggie! Maggie, where are you? Where's Ty? Is he nearby? Let me talk—"

"Laurie, Ty's not with me... what makes you think he is with me? Is Ty missing?" sounding confused with all the strange questions Laurie launches at her.

"Listen, I just called to let Ty know that everything is fine and working out as planned and not to worry about me."

Laurie begins to sob, "Maggie, where's my husband?"

"Laurie, I hate to cut you short, but I have got to run. My plane leaves in two minutes."

"Maggie! Maggie!"

"Sorry, hun, got to run..."

Laurie heard nothing but a dial tone, and she broke down into heavy sobs.

Time stood still as Ty turned the page to read the dictation from the past in a slight whisper as if it were a mystery about to be revealed. Moe listened closely, even though after all the years, he remembered.

... It was a cold and clear night. We had read the Word of God and had a wonderful discussion about the meaning of prophecy. All of a sudden... Moe started shaking! Huber and I thought he was having a physical problem, but to our surprise, Moe began loudly speaking words about the future. Huber nudged me strongly to get a pencil and paper to take it down. I jumped up and ran to the table drawer, where I found my writing tools. I took down as much as I could.

> **"I, the Lord God desire that no man perish. It is**
> **My will that My creation worship Me. Nature**
> **will. The birds, the animals, they know Me,**
> **and they follow My natural pattern, but**
> **man... My crowning creation, they resist Me**
> **in ways I mourn over..."**

Moe's eyes followed Ty with great interest. His arthritic knuckles rubbed together as he clasped his weathered hands.

> **"I, the Lord, have heard the cries of bloodshed on**
> **this mountain, and have seen the evil intent**
> **of man's heart and the poison they create that**
> **destroys life—life I have given."**

Ty stops midway, slightly folding the journal. Looking up at Moe, he asks, "God is speaking about the moonshiners, isn't He?" Ty had heard from residents of Hidden Creek the summary of the town's history and various details of its early beginnings.

Moe nods slowly, affirming the question. He adjusts in his chair, knowing full well what Ty was about to read. His eyes growing wide and serious, Ty looks down at the journal again to continue reading.

**"I have also heard the cries of my servants, and
by their faith in Me, I shall deliver them. I will
bring about providence to the city below, but
it will come by a purging of evil. It will turn
the hearts of the people toward Me, and then,
they shall know that I am God."**

Ty trembles inside and bites his lip. A million questions pop into his mind. He glances over at Moe, who has stepped over to the fire to stir it once again. Silence fills the room... *He knows. Moe is certain this is the time. But why has God chosen me to carry out this providence? An outsider? Why now, with my wife expecting? And my job?*

In a hushed-like tone, Ty asks, "Is this the time, Moe?"

"Sure'n is, sir," stirring the stew in the pot above the fire and then tapping the wooden spoon against the edge. He reaches and pours Ty a cup of fresh coffee.

"Moe, how do you know?"

"The Holy Ghost, sir. He spoke to me's heart at the back of the schoolhouse on the wings of the wind. I's been waiting a long time, sir, but He, the Lord, is faithful."

"Wings of the wind?" Ty asks with a perplexed look.

The old man looks up, face beaming with "the glory," as he raises his right hand. "The Holy Ghost blows where He wills. The wind blows where it wills. You's feel it, but ya don't see it. So 'tis with the Holy Ghost." With tears in his eyes, Moe lowers his hand.

Nicodemus. This is how Nicodemus must have felt that night with Jesus. The scene shook Ty to his core. The closeness to God that Moe exhibited was convicting him of his "everydayness" relationship that he personally had. Had God been speaking all along, and he hadn't listened? What had he missed? An opportunity? A witness? All this... now?

Finishing his bowl of stew, Moe grabs several large, blue cotton blankets and prepares a padded bed on the floor by the fire. Moe lies down, says some prayers, and quietly utters, "Goodnight, sir."

An hour passes, and the fire slowly dissolves into hot glowing embers. Ty sits and stares into the coals. He senses the closeness of God in a different way as he considers all that is happening.

Yes, something truly wonderful is in the works. I have left everything. My wife. My children. My job. God has brought me here for a providence He is bringing. He sent Moe to help me. And I listened.

Ty rubs his forehead. He is growing tired. And then the voice of the Lord comes again, this time giving him comfort:

"And everyone who has left houses or brothers or sisters or father or mother or wife or children or fields for my sake…"

Deputy Will North jiggled the change in his pocket, standing in the neighboring Percy City Police Headquarters, some seventy miles west of Hidden Creek. He was expecting a call back from Sheriff McMurphy while sipping on the strong coffee that should have been thrown out hours earlier.

Recently, Will had uncovered a lead in the Walker case: a local merchant recognized Ty Walker's photo and mentioned that he had purchased gear typical for a camping trip—things like a backpack, rain gear, and matches. Another retailer believed she saw Walker buying staples for a stay of about a month or so, but she wasn't sure. Deputy North was glad to have any information. He had been searching for over a week without a clue, and he was weary of dead ends.

The phone ringing makes North jump as Sheriff Tubal of Percy City reaches for it.

"Hello. Sheriff Tubal here. Yes... mmm hmm... North, it's for you," he says with a strong southern drawl and hands him the phone.

"Hello... Yeah... Hey, Mac... I've got a lead."

Chapter 16
Face of Moses

At four-thirty in the morning, a cast-iron skillet was atop the old antique stove, sizzling. Oliver Wendell Huber, an early riser, had beaten sunrise again. He believed that there was no sense in losing the day, even though it was dark, and for more years than he could remember, he kept the record going. Oliver hummed happy tunes beside the stove, stirring grits and onions to prevent them from sticking, while cooking bacon in the skillet on the opposite side.

Still in his long johns and hat, he grabs his worn overalls off the kitchen table and puts them on beside the stove. He was particularly happy because this was his fishing day. Once a week, he and Rastus, his faithful fishing buddy, went out to fish while a young man by the name of Tommy Battles took care of the launch.

After filling his belly with bacon, eggs, grits, and onions, and his special hash, which had a little of this and a lot of that, Oliver steps outside his cabin, putting on his coat, pushing back his hat, looks at the sky, and hollers for his companion of ten years.

"Rat! Rat! Come on, boy!"

Around the corner by a woodpile shed, a large, hairy, black and gray mutt comes running and yapping a short, sharp-pitched bark. He begins jumping at Oliver and nearly knocks him down.

"Quit it, Rat!" Oliver chides. He leans over to grab his fishing gear, box, and stringer while fighting off the loving advances of his faithful partner, who is now licking him on the face and ears.

Rat backs up, plops down on his rear, and wags his tail, creating a thumping sound against a shed.

Smiling, Oliver pats him on the head. "That's a what I like—a dog tail with a happy ending!" The attention made Rat whine and yowl.

"C'mon boy, let's go."

They meandered down to the launch to their favorite skiff, Number 5. It was wider than the others and had padded seats with holders on the sides for poles, and a small five-horsepower motor.

Rat immediately jumps into the skiff and heads for the bow, where Oliver had built a platform for him to sit. Oliver primes the gas bulb and pulls twice to start the motor. Sputtering along at a slow rate, he steers the boat toward Frog Rock (a large, rock formation resembling a toad squatting on the bank), where he knew the fishing was good this time of year.

Rat, like a statue, sits on the bow of the boat, bites at the air with his ears flopping. Every so often, he howls, provoking Oliver to tap him on the back to hush him up. As Oliver slows down to where he plans to bait, Rat's excitement intensifies.

"Rat! You ol' codger! Hush! Don't ya tell 'em we're a comin!"

Rat moans with the command, wagging his tail furiously.

Oliver drops anchors on both ends of the skiff and starts to fiddle with his reels and poles. On the back side, two poles are rigged up with the cheeseballs he'd mixed the night before with his special recipe of bread and chopped chicken liver. On the other side, he cast two lines to bottom fish, cranking the tension just so to see the slightest bite. Then, leaning back, he waits and relaxes. Pushing back his hat and glancing up the face of the mountain, Oliver sees something he hadn't seen in years—smoke billowing from the old hermit's cabin.

"Now I wonder, Rat, who'd be way up yonder," rubbing the big dog's head and ears. "I just wonder." He pauses in thought and then speaks to Rat, "When we git back in, we'll make a call to the Sheriff. Won't we, Rat? You remind me, won't ya, Rat?" Rat responds with another soft whine.

SHERIFF MCMURPHY STEERED the old but well-kept patrol car up the mountain road, turning right at mile marker sixty-three onto a firm dirt road with grass growing in the middle of it. There was no evidence of tire tracks, possibly due to the recent heavy rain. Luckily, today was a little drier than the first part of the week, so sliding was not a problem. Mac maneuvered slowly, looking for any clue of car traffic in any of the side pathways or small brush.

None. Nothing! Mac drove on, determined.

Up ahead, the dirt road split into a "Y," but Mac knew the "Y" was really the beginning of a large circle. He knew because he had hunted here an eon ago. Mac turned right at the "Y" which was a closer route to the trail that led to the old hermit's cabin. The cabin was his initial destination since he received a call from Huber at the launch the previous evening.

Been a while since I've been up here, he thought, remembering a past hunting trip with his father some forty years prior. *Father! A fine man with a contagious smile. A praying man. Prayed for this sad sack of a son many times before he died. Never found fault with anything or anyone.*

Mac sighed heavily, thinking over the years of being a cop and finding fault with everything. *Robberies. Drunks. Fights. The kids.* He sighed again. *Kids had gone crazy with the drugs, alcohol, and sadly, suicide.*

Seeing something unusual, he slides to a halt. To his passenger side, he could see what appears to be a vehicle trail through some brush. He immediately jumps out to investigate.

"Yep. Somebody's driven through here. Could only be a four-wheel drive to do it, though." He walks about fifty yards into the woods when suddenly he sees the camouflage net. Removing the net, he finds a black Roughrider that he recognizes.

"Ty Walker's," stating out loud in a curious tone.

Since the door was locked, he peered through the glass, seeing much of nothing. From the passenger side window, he examines the ignition switch. *No keys... nothing unusual.* He considers calling it in, but he realizes quickly that he's out of range for his patrol radio to reach base. As soon as he gets back into range, he'll have the vehicle checked further.

Mac, following his instincts and years of training, does a perimeter check twenty yards around the Roughrider. Nothing. Moving farther out to a distance of fifty yards, he finds one broken limb leading to the cabin trailhead about a mile or so toward the mountain range. Walking back to his patrol car, he considers going to get help. He sits in the driver's seat for fifteen minutes, wrestling with the idea of what to do.

Could it be Walker at the cabin? If it is, what in the world is he doing? Maybe if it is, Ty may be in trouble. Not a good idea going off into the hills without anyone knowing where I am. It's a mile or so to the trail or what is left of a trail, and then uphill hiking to the cabin is going to be a task. Been a while since I experienced some serious exercise. He looks down at the pudginess of his uniform. *As soon as I get back, this blubber has got to start coming off.*

Mac decides to leave a hand-drawn map on the dash of the

patrol car, informing others of where he's going. Patting his stomach, he mutters under his breath, "I can't believe I'm doing this."

Rick Rider smiles broadly as he welcomes and extends his hand to Sid Brumley in the presence of a crowded room filled with reporters from several counties and towns. The scene buzzed with excitement. Nothing like this had ever happened in Hidden Creek.

"Ladies and gentlemen of the press, this is the Owner and Chief Editor of the *Hidden Creek Daily News*, Sid Brumley. Mr. Brumley will fill you in on all the details and updates on our recent release of the Walker embezzlement case and his current disappearance from Hidden Creek." Rick's tone was serious, but he was feeling in control of the power trip he was experiencing.

Sid approaches the set-up podium somewhat timidly. He was not used to all this attention, and it was making him nervous. Still, it was his responsibility, and he quickly shifted gears into a serious personality.

"I welcome every one of you to Hidden Creek. We all know why we are here today, so I will let you start the ball rolling by answering your questions," he says in his deepest voice.

Hands start to go up all over the room!

Huffing and puffing three hours later, Mac stops to rest and catch his breath. Though slightly cool, he had already shed his coat from the hike. After catching his wind, Mac traverses slowly the final leg of the climb.

Nearing the cabin, he sees no one outside, although a stream of smoke pours from the chimney. The windows are unshaded, and an axe leans against the wall. He notices wood chippings where someone had been chopping. Mac hesitates before moving forward, hiding behind brush and fallen logs. It's difficult for Mac to approach without being seen.

The front door opens with a creak, causing Mac to jump. The figure before him turns, and Mac catches a glimpse of the man's face. He can tell it's a black man.

Moonshiner? reasoned Mac. *Nah. Not this high up...*

The subject grabs the axe and turns in the opposite direction from Mac.

Moe? Moe Wilson? What is he doing here?

The situation was getting more confusing by the minute. He waited. Mac watched Moe chop wood for several minutes until the large man laid down the axe and began to carry an armload of wood to the cabin.

"This is the time," Mac whispers to himself, coming out into the open, gun drawn. He signals Moe to stand still. Moe freezes abruptly and drops the wood.

"Moe, what are you doing here?"

"Officer, I's here to help Mr. Walker."

"Ty Walker?"

"Yes, sir. He's inside, sir. Praying, sir."

Mac was stunned. The word "praying" was the last thing he expected.

"Come on! Let's go inside and get to the bottom of this."

Moe opens the creaking door, and both men step inside. By the fireplace, Ty Walker is kneeling over a large stump made into an altar. His head was covered with a shawl of sorts. He makes no effort to get up or look up. Moe walks over and touches Ty's back.

"Mr. Walker, Officer Mac is here. He wants to know what's

going on. 'Tis the Lord's will that he does, sir?" he inquires, leaving Officer Mac looking puzzled.

"Have a seat, Mac," Ty's voice gently whispers. Ty doesn't get up or uncover his face.

"Is something wrong, Ty?" Mac asks, noticing his reluctance to move. "What is all this about? You disappear. Your wife and kids are worried sick, and the town is in an uproar about you and some money they allege you stole from the county. I am your friend, Ty... You can tell me." Mac blurts out in a pleading tone.

"I will tell you this, my good friend. I have never lied to you. I have come here by God's direction. I have missed my family, and I did not take any money from the county or anyone else."

"So, when are you coming back to refute all these allegations?"

Ty takes a deep breath and begins to whisper a prayer.

Mac looks at Moe, who by now is also praying. Mac repositions himself in his chair, showing signs of discomfort with the scene before him.

After a few moments, Ty speaks. "Twenty-one days, says the Lord, and all will be clean."

"Twenty-one days?" repeats Mac. "Hidden Creek will be in bedlam in twenty-one days with the rumors and the press! They are—"

"Officer Christopher Mayhew McMurphy..." Ty recites with authority.

That stunned Mac in his seat! No one alive except his wife knew his christened name, and yet, Ty gave it exactly!

"You are not to tell anyone that you have seen me. Twenty-one days are proclaimed."

Ty rises slowly, turning to face Mac, who instinctively stands as well. He uncovers his head, and Mac gasps in fear, trembling, and on the verge of collapsing! Ty's face radiates with a brilliance like that of Moses!

Chapter 17

Town Gone Crazy

AJ Petry floored the pedal of the rusted Chevrolet, while it spewed smoke out the back of the car. He and his friends, Jordan Scott, "Scooter" Michaels, and "Daredevil" Derek, laughed hysterically after AJ sent a mailbox flying with the bumper of his car. They were freewheeling and looking for anything to get into. Trouble especially. All of them were high from smoking the best weed in the area they could find. After skipping school, their activities included hanging out at Crossman's Corner, smoking their stash, destroying mailboxes (four, so far), turning over old man Nickles' outhouse, and wheeling a few circles in Mrs. Manson's prize-winning rosebush garden area, which this time of year had no flowers. Still, they destroyed several of her prized quality bushes. They were invincible. Nothing could stop them... or so they thought.

Blue flashing lights in the rear mirror interrupted their escapade.

After coming to a stop, Officer Will North radios in the tag and then proceeds cautiously toward the car with his hand on his gun. He has no idea why the car that passed him was so erratic on the road. Tapping gently on the window, AJ rolls it down, while the rest of the crew goes silent.

Officer North immediately smells the smoke and orders all of them out of the car and has them line up with their backs to the side of it.

Scooter Michaels starts snickering.

"What's so funny, young man?" asks North.

"You look like one of those Deputy Do-rights!" he responds with a loud laugh. The rest of the young men also burst into loud laughter. Amid the silliness, Scooter adds, "Probably running a checkpoint chickee!" At that, they nearly fell onto the ground!

"All right—names. And I need to see your license," pointing to AJ.

After scanning the license, North nods. "It's up to date."

"Turn around, Mr. Petry. You are under arrest for driving under the influence."

The others begin fussing loudly, spitting towards him.

At that, North orders AJ, "Roll down the front window halfway down!" He handcuffs AJ and Scooter to the driver's door open window using one wrist of each. They complain that it hurts. Turning to Jordan and Derek, North commands, "Now it's you two to the back door the same way! And stop your bellyaching!"

Will walks back to the patrol car and radios the part-time deputized citizens that he needs some backup to cart the four young men back to the station. After radioing in for help, he watches them try to kick gravel toward his car as they continue spitting and yelling.

While shaking his head in disbelief at the scene before him, he mutters, "This town's gone crazy! It's like the Devil is dropping a bucket of crazy!"

~

Across town, Mildred Piper, a member of Community Church, was deep in conversation with Lily Mae Roberts, who attends Mount Ridge Baptist Church.

"Lily, you would not believe what I heard! Ty Walker may have taken some money from our church treasury. You know how Pastor Stoddard is always asking for more 'tithing' and all that most of the time? And he is a money counter at the church? Ty could dip into it at any time!"

"No! You don't say!" biting into a cream-filled doughnut as juicy as the gossip. "I had heard he'd run off to Europe with that hussy Maggie Stewart."

"Oh, Lily! That's old news!" she said in exasperation to her gossip companion.

Pete Hammon, a retired city employee, strolled into Rhodes Hardware, wasting time because he was bored with nothing to do. Tom Rhodes, owner of the established business, smiles broadly at Pete. He knew Pete was loitering to pass time, and he loved for him to come in because he was such a character with the jokes. The old-timers in the corner, with a checker game in progress, enjoyed him equally.

"Pete," Tom calls out as he wipes the counter.

"Hey, Tom. Fellers." The old men in the corner looked up and grinned, waving briefly before resuming their game.

"What's up, Pete?" Tom asks, waiting for the joke of the day.

"Ah, nothing much," reaching for a cold drink. "But now that you ask, I heard a good one." Immediately, everyone stopped what they were doing. Nobody could tell a joke like Pete, and they were not going to miss a single word.

"I heard that the Governor was looking for a personal runner to gather funds for his re-election campaign. A member of his staff recommended a 'Walker.' The Guv' told the staff member he didn't need a 'walker' but a 'runner.' The staff member argued for a spell with the Guv' and continued to say that he needed a 'Walker.' The Guv' frustrated said, "No! Didn't you hear me? I need a runner who can gather some large campaign money fast!" The young staff member, completely exhausted from arguing, reached into his briefcase, pulled out a document, and handed it to the Governor. After the Guv' read the letter, he put it down and turned to the staff member and said, "You're right! Get the staff car ready. We're going to Hidden Creek. Best 'Walker' I ever heard of."

Everyone exploded in laughter.

RICK RIDER WAS DELIRIOUS. Deliriously happy. He had made connections with personnel in Nebraska who gave him more choice details of Ty Walker, his background, his criminal activity, jail time, everything. There was every rock uncovered about Walker's past. Every detail hit the print board with the speed of light.

People knew personal details of his past, like how Ty Walker, at the age of thirteen, was arrested for shoplifting a watch in a department store, although he claimed a friend placed the watch in his pocket without his knowledge. Another incident involved an Article 15 reprimand in military service for drunk and disorderly conduct, resulting in a pushing match with a base policeman. Walker was demoted accordingly. Rider also found the story about the stillborn death of a son, which he purposely left out due to the possible sympathy Walker might receive. Rider had two things in mind with all this digging—to be moved up in career somewhere other than Hidden Creek, and to display the hypocrisy of the Christian faith that he despised deeply. Rick had a slang name for all of them since his teen years—Church Molesters!

He would say, "Nothing but phony church molesters who were never satisfied with money and always wanting more! Instead of giving... all they do is take, take, take! And fake? Yeah, fake!" Rick's father "professed" at one time to be a Christian, and then he ran off and left him and his mother for another woman, ironically, one from the church. His mother was branded as a "divorcee" by the church and told not to ever come back. "Dirty, stinking, Church Molesters!" he shouted.

Career aspirations, however, were coming true in Rider's life. He had been contacted by two major papers and a high-level broadcasting station. He decided to let them "bite at the bit" for a while before his final answer because he knew it could turn out to be more money. Besides, he was having the time of his life, basking in all the attention and prestige. Rider liked to say, "The money will come. Big money!"

Laurie Walker was limited to the house. Her ankles and legs were swollen, and the doctor had ordered bed rest with very little work, if any at all. Some friends from the church came regularly to help with the cooking, cleaning, and the kids. And when they arrived, Laurie asked that they not talk about all the bad rumors circulating around town. She knew about them already in indirect ways.

The trash man refused to pick up trash. Church members helped by taking her trash to their homes instead. The newsboy quit throwing the Walker's paper by order of his father not to associate with "those kinds of people." Graffiti found its way on the white picket fence Ty had installed to border the front yard, decrying horrible things. Pastor Stoddard and his wife cleaned it daily, but the next day the words would reappear as if by magic.

Two nights prior, Laurie had to call the police to report some people who had crashed a brick through a bedroom window with a note attached that read:

RIGHTEOUS HYPOCRITE!

At the moment, Laurie lay on the couch listening to relaxing music. Her mind confused, but strangely gaining peace over the whole situation. It was as if she were drawing power from the Lord Jesus, a source of comfort, encouragement, and strength. Someone was praying for her, and she could tell without an iota of doubt!

At Casey's bar, the regulars lounged around, sitting on barstools, smoking and drinking heavily. The room had a hazy atmosphere and a jukebox that blared the latest country tune. The sound of billiards cracked in the corner from the lone pool table. Ellie Ramsey, a part-time helper in her twenties, washed mugs, plates, and silverware to the right of the bar counter. She was beginning to grow sick of all the talk that had been happening in the bar of late.

"Yeah, I heard that ol' Walker feller was the biggest thief in the history of the state of Nebraska," pipes Ernest Gilmore, a local good-for-nothing.

"Probably in the state of Tennessee, too," chuckles Bubba McCormick, a local farmer from the south end of Hidden Creek. "Hey, babe, get me 'nuther coldun."

"I'm not your babe," Ellie snorts, taking her time in getting Bubba a beer.

"So, Ellie, what do you think about this Christian feller going back to the pig's mire?" Bubba asks, showing his rotten bottom teeth.

Ellie felt a little sick to her stomach as she mutters, "Don't know if he's done anything wrong. Can't make a judgement before all the facts are out."

"All the facts!" roars Ernest. "Honey, that no good hypocrite took all the money, alright? And he took that woman with him for some extra comfort, if you know what I mean!"

In defense, Ellie sternly objects and blurts out, "Ernest, you have no basis to accuse him of that! Now hush up before I get Elroy to show you the door!"

At that, Ernest took a long drag on his cigarette and grew silent. He wanted no part of Big Boy Elroy—a huge, muscled-up giant of a man—in his business.

"Why are you defending this Walker fellow anyway?" Joanne Cassidy asks, joining the conversation.

She was dead drunk and hadn't said much all night. She pushed her stringy red hair back from her face, which had fallen over her eyes for most of the evening, only lifting it when she wanted to sip a drink.

"What is he? Some kind of saint?" she pushes out, slurring her words.

"Yeah, Ellie. Why are you defending this so-called Christian?" Lonnie Tucker interjects as he and his brother Melvin stop shooting pool.

"Yeah, why?" Melvin chimes in.

Meekly, Ellie speaks, "He's an okay man..." Ellie says softly, her voice trailing off as she begins to feel the pressure of being outnumbered. Deep down, she knew why she felt this way. Years ago, Principal Tyrel Walker took time to tutor her in math, a subject she had struggled horribly. Had it not been for him, she would not have earned her high school diploma. Ellie stared around the room at the many faces glaring back at her.

"Well, come on, young lady! Spill it or zip it..." Ernest spouts in reply to the quiet-faced Ellie. She turns around and resumes washing as the patrons begin to snicker.

"Christians. Ha! Do-gooders who can't even take care of themselves, much less somebody out there who really needs help," says Lonnie. Melvin nods in agreement.

"Beam in the eye," Joanne says drunkenly, wetting her finger and pointing upward. "That's what it 'tis..."

"Tell ya what. If I had run off with some cute redhead, my wife woulda given me a beam all right. Right upside my head," Bubba interjects, snickering.

On impulse, Ernest scolded, "Bubba, you couldn't find another woman who'd have you to run off with!"

Everyone in the bar burst into laughter except Ellie, who was trying to keep her tears in check. She knew it was going to be a rough evening.

With all this foolishness, it is going to be a long night, she thought to herself.

Chapter 18
Strange Calm

Tornadoes have a peculiar personality of their own. Before they strike and destroy, a strange calm usually settles in, and then, without warning, except for the oncoming rush of wind, chaos explodes. Hidden Creek was acquainted with tornadoes. Being in tornado alley, they were relatively common from early spring to late fall.

Eighteen years prior, an extreme tornado ripped the town apart, roaring down Main Street and throwing debris everywhere. All the folks in town who remembered that massive cloud recalled one distinct fact—though the weather signs were displayed, a strange quietness first settled across the land, a sort of trickery.

It was calm in Hidden Creek. Eerie calm.

Deputy North, now in charge of the station due to the absence of Sheriff McMurphy, creaked back and forth at his office desk with his feet propped up. His face, stuck in the sports section of *The Daily*, was intensely interested in the college football section. He was especially engrossed in the article about the Tennessee

Volunteers game. During the past week, his work and duties had become so dull and uneventful that he began looking for things to do—painting, repairing the broken sink in the men's room, and volunteering for school crossings even though he despised it at other times.

No one occupied the cells. The four teens arrested earlier in the previous week had bail posted for them by family members. In a way, North was glad they were gone—they were mouthy toward him but scared by the adjoining foul prisoner that week, Lake Lasota. He was a real rough character. Prior charges ranged from burglary, attempted sexual assault, assault on an officer, and numerous other incidents. Lasota was an animal in jail, constantly cursing, swearing, and screaming at anyone in earshot. Lasota also banged the food tray against the bars, irritating everyone. He growled constantly at the complaining youth. Having difficulty in containing the wild man, the State ordered a transfer to the Farmington Penitentiary for holding until his cases appeared. The four high school teens in the next cell got a birds-eye view of what the bad people were like in prison. North hoped they were scared straight to never break the law again.

Deputy North put down the newspaper and stared out the front window at the very little movement, even on Main Street. Rubbing his face with his hands, he thought, *Nothing could be this quiet or calm in town. Even "Greasy Trotter," the town drunk and weekly pick up, had gone on the wagon from his drinking. About the only action this week was the fire at Glory Days Retirement Home. The entire building was lost, but no one was injured. All twenty-eight patrons were transferred to Golden Oaks in Sipley until the repairs were made.* His chair began creaking again in the silent station.

The ringing phone made Will North jump and nearly fall backwards in his chair.

"Hidden Creek Police Department," barks Will with a breathless voice.

"Will? Mac. Just checking in to see how things are going. Everything okay?"

"Mac, it's good to hear anything right now. The town is so quiet and dull. I'm wondering if I'm even needed!"

"You are, Will, you are," reassuring the deputy.

"Mac, are you feeling any better? You haven't missed but a few days in the years that I've been here," voicing his concern about his friend for six years. "Have you been to see Doc Waters yet?"

"I'm fine, Will. Just need some time off, that's all. Job shock, overtime, neglecting wife..." He rattles on a bit more, "You know how it is."

Will understood this on a personal level. Being on the police force can be rewarding, but also hassling. Enough to drive a person over the edge, and family, too. Will's ex-wife, Sally, had divorced him three years prior, moved out of state with the children, and remarried. Of all things, she got hitched to a stress counselor who was home every evening at 5:30 p.m. No guns, little, if any stress, and someone who would give her the personal communication she craved, which she constantly criticized him about during their years of marriage.

Still, Mac's absence remains confusing to Will. Mac has been a steady, unnerving, strong officer of the law for thirty-two years. It all began when he drove up to the mountain and came back a different person—shaken. He has been off for four days, and it sounds like he was considering not coming back.

"Will, are you still there?" Mac queries after a long period of silence.

"Yeah, Mac, just thinking. What happened up on the hill?" shooting straight from the hip with the question that plagued his mind.

"I..." his voice was breaking. "I can't discuss it... You wouldn't... You wouldn't understand."

"But, Mac, we're friends!"

"I know we are, Will. That's why I will need you to be my friend and not ask. I need to go. I'll be in touch tomorrow."

"Later then, Mac." Hanging up the phone, Will returned to his newspaper, still baffled by the whole ordeal.

Mac looks across his living room toward a shelf of books lining the top of his fireplace. He walks over, brushes off a layer of thick dust, and picks up one book. Opening its cover to the first page, he finds a written note:

To Mac,

A gift from me to you.
I love you!

Your Wife,
Mabel

P.S.
Make sure you
read page 884.

Turning slowly to page 884, he reads out loud:

"In the beginning was the Word and the Word was with God, and the Word was God."

— JOHN 1:1

GLASSES RATTLED AT MOREY'S DINER, a local favorite for townspeople to go and have a decent lunch. The floors were checkered in green and white squares with padded green booths giving the impression of a fifties flashback. Healthy plants hung in various places all over the diner, and cute placards with funny quotes were strategically placed where the plants couldn't cover them up. Small jukebox flip-cards hung by each table if patrons wanted to pick out a tune while waiting for lunch to be served. A large jukebox centered against the far wall, at present, bellowed out a country song with a twangy tune.

In the corner booth, Rick Rider sat nervously picking his nails. He was expecting Nettie. A daring move to meet with her in public, yet he needed one more detail about "the story" that had taken the town by storm. Besides, she had been bugging him to no end about being seen with him in public, and to pacify her, Rick had agreed. Deep down, he hated the idea. People might get the wrong impression about the two of them together. Swallowing his ego, he thought, what could it hurt seeing that he was going to leave town anyway when he accepted an offer?

The front door jingles with the sound of small bells, jolting Rick Rider back to reality, and Nettie enters dressed to the nines, her hair fixed and her confidence boosted by having dropped about ten pounds. Swinging her purse slightly, she walks over to Rick's table, swaying her hips.

In a rare moment, Rick catches himself admiring her looks as he laughs to himself inside. *She is starting to look nice. She would be a decent woman if it weren't for being the big nose and mouth of the town. As soon as I am on my way up, she will be out.*

"Hi, Rick," Nettie greets, taking a seat next to him, while looking around to see if anyone was watching them.

"It was very nice of you to ask me to join you for lunch. Surprising, but nice. I have always known that deep down you are a really, really, nice guy!" Nettie leans in toward Rick, smiling.

Rick smiles back, gritting his teeth slightly, as he thinks... *If you only knew, Sweety-pie, how nice I really am...*

Chapter 19
The Invitation

"Got everything?" inquires Ty.

"Yes, sir," puffs Moe, picking up a small pack with water, some food, and a raincoat in case of a downpour.

"Here, take this," says Ty, handing Moe a note. "This is what the Lord has commanded. No matter what, this must be posted all over town. Hand out as many invitations as you can. Please put them in front of stores and on park benches. If a store cashier allows you to place some on their counters, do so. Answer no questions."

"I's know not all the answers, sir. That has been revealed to you only from the Lord."

"Stay in town only through Friday, and then return here to be with me. Leave late at night or early in the morning to avoid being followed. Here is the money for the copies, for food, and gas if needed. The Lord shall give you strength." Ty reaches out and touches Moe's shoulder.

"Well glory!!!" Moe the servant of the Lord exclaims, feeling an incredible surge of power from Ty's hand. Tears well up in his eyes from the experience as he opens the cabin door and steps outside into the brisk air.

"Keep praying, sir... Pray!"

"I will, Moe," waving to his companion.

MAC McMURPHY WEEPS UNCONTROLLABLY beside the couch in his living room while his Christian wife, Mabel, looks on with tears streaming down her cheeks. Years of pent-up frustration over the fact that her husband had not yielded to the Lord spilled forth into tears of joy. Mac, broken before her, verbally pours out his numerous sins, his failures as a husband, his lack of concern for God Himself—everything. Nearby, a Bible lies open, and beside it, a mangled and crushed pack of cigarettes.

Drawing close to her husband, Mabel bends to her knees and places her hands on his back, feeling his sobs of inner pain and release. Though his confessions seem to be tearing her husband apart, she rejoices deeply over the fact that God had finally gotten through to him, showing gratitude to God for His long-suffering with Mac and His faithfulness to her prayers. She also praised God for Tyrel Walker, who single-handedly had brought her husband many miles closer to the Lord during the past five years that Ty had been in Hidden Creek. She marveled at God's power over whatever had happened to Mac up in the hills because he had not been the same since that day. And now this. Sweet victory!

After a long period of time, the sobbing stopped. Finally broken, peace came. Peace. Mac turned to his beloved wife and hugged her passionately. They stayed in each other's arms for a long time, both crying and laughing. Mabel could see the change. Mac's entire appearance was beaming.

"Mac... I am so happy for you!" bursting out the words. They hug again.

"I know the Lord works in mysterious ways. I know that He has saved you, and I praise my—and your—Lord Jesus for His grace."

In her exuberance, she adds, "And I must know what happened on the mountain that has brought this on today!"

Mac looked at her glowingly. "Mabel, I now know what you have been trying to get through my thick skull for years. If I had only known!"

"You do now, honey... That's all that matters."

"About the mountain Mabel..."

"Yes?" drawing closer to him with her eyes showing intense interest.

"You shall know very, very soon. I promise you."

BRAKES FROM MOE WILSON'S pickup truck squeak to a halt in front of the We-Print-It shop at about three o'clock in the afternoon.

Earlier on, Moe had spent the better part of the day hiking down the trail and locating his truck. Afterward, he drove home, ate a quick lunch, and showered. Then he dressed in his best go-a-meeting clothes.

Stepping into We-Print-It, Ned Gilmore, the owner, looks at Moe with a curious glare. It struck Ned as it was only Tuesday, and Moe was dressed up. Ignoring his instincts to question him, he got down to the more important matter—business.

"Can I help you, Moe?"

"Yes, sir, sure'n can."

"Have you got any money, Moe?" he asks in a derogatory way, knowing full well Moe was basically poor and rarely spent money on anything but essential needs.

"I'm sure, sir, you'n ask everybody the same question," Moe responds, showing Ned some currency in his hand.

Red-faced and embarrassed, Ned wheels around to Sam Redman, who was sipping on a cup of coffee, and states loudly,

"I hear, Sam, the county may have an early berry season next year." Then turning back to Moe, he snips quickly, "You like berry pickin', don't ya, Moe?" Sam Redman chuckles, almost spilling his coffee, as he watches the scene unfold before him.

Moe stood still. His facial expression never wavered as the Lord gave him strength to maintain composure. Ned Gilmore's grandfather, Will, was one of the moonshiners who hung his parents and was never charged.

"I need some copies made," Moe replies in a controlled tone.

"He needs some copies, Sam. Reckon how many he needs... say one or two?" blurting the question with a smirk. "We have a minimum limit of five, or is that too much for someone like you?" he adds quickly, while Sam chuckles once again.

"One thousand, sir."

At that, Ned gulps, nearly knocking off a counter display. "One thousand? You sure? That is close to two hundred dollars, even with the discount! What are you doing, Moe? Running for Mayor of Hidden Creek?" Sam shakes his head in disbelief.

"Here's what I's want printed. I's be back by tomorrow to pick them up. And keep this notice to yourself until tomorrow."

Ned examines the message, exhibiting a peculiar expression. "Your money, Moe. And speaking of money, this is the time you pay. Up front."

Sam giggles again, because in all the years he had known Ned, he had never made a single customer pay up front. And the idea of keeping it quiet... well, that was ridiculous.

Moe carefully counts the money into Ned's hand, collects his change, and walks out without another word.

Sam and Ned explode into spontaneous laughter as the door jingles behind him.

Laurie Walker sat on the front porch swing, watching a beautiful, calm sunset ending the day, while she hummed a rock-a-bye tune to the infant who kicked and stretched her womb. Peaceful. It was truly peaceful around the Walker household. The harassment had tapered off, and the phone had stopped its endless ringing. The church had raised a special offering to help alleviate the burden of food and bills coming in without Ty's income.

"Ty, I know you're out there," she whispers as the baby kicks. "Yes, you know your daddy is out there, too," she says, rubbing her stomach. "I feel your prayers. I have learned that wherever you are, the Lord is in control, and you are in His hands, which are a lot larger than mine. I just want you to know that whatever God is doing with you, follow His will."

Laurie continues to rock and sing as she enjoys the peace. Sweet peace.

A little before ten in the morning, Moe Wilson drives up to We-Print-It, only to meet a gathering of townspeople hanging around. Ned and Sam had spread the tale about Moe and the message, and they were there to check if it was true or not. Of course, *The Daily* had caught wind of the rumor.

Rick Rider paces impatiently back and forth in front of the door, which is set to open at ten o'clock. As soon as he spots Moe's truck drive up, he grabs his recorder, ready to catch every word.

"What's this all about, Moe?" he asks, shoving a microphone into his face.

Moe, refusing to utter a word, politely brushes off the mic.

"Where's Ty Walker? You know you may be harboring a criminal. Give us the story!" Rider fires off question after question to no avail.

Moe works his way through the curious bodies surrounding the print shop and enters. Inside, he flashes his claim ticket and proceeds to carry the two boxes to the back of his truck. Rick Rider follows Moe in and out of the shop, asking questions at a machine gun rate while Moe remains mute.

After the continuous haranguing from Rider, Moe opens a box and hands Rider the first copy, who snatches it quickly from Moe's hand. Still without a word, Moe then passes a handful to the closest person, who in turn starts spreading them to others.

Then Moe steps out into the road and raises his hands towards Heaven, declaring in a loud voice:

"Tell them! Tell them! Tell them all who will listen! Tell them! Tell them all!"

Rick Rider's face was glued to the copy, which read:

TO: HIDDEN CREEK TOWNSPEOPLE

AN INVITATION THAT IS URGENT FOR YOU TO HEED. AS IT WAS IN THE DAYS OF SODOM AND GOMORRAH WHEN LOT RECEIVED A WORD TO COME OUT OF THEM, SO TOO, HERE NOW, DOES THE LORD REQUEST THE SAME OF YOU, THE PEOPLE OF HIDDEN CREEK. GOD IS FAITHFUL. HE DOES NOT LIE.

WHEN: SATURDAY, JANUARY 22ND
WHERE: ASSEMBLE AT EAGLE POINT ROCK EAST OF HUBER'S CAMP

TIME: 7:00 PM
WHO: ALL WHO HEAR HIS VOICE

TYREL WALKER

Rick Rider was perplexed. For him, it was a rare moment.

Chapter 20
Ingathering

"Ron! Ron! Is that machine ever going to finish?" snorted Sid Brumley. His side ached from the lack of sleep and the stress of covering the news of Ty Walker. He had Ron cranking out print since 3:00 a.m., and Sid himself was rolling them as fast as they dried. There was a full cover story on the life of Tyrel Walker, his family, career, work at church, everything. And most importantly, his disappearance, with every view, angle, and guess at what it might be or mean.

Saturday 7:00 a.m.

Hidden Creek was caught up in the message given to them by Walker, and it was making Sid a very rich and important man. The trophy for story of the year was in his back pocket, and no one could take it away from him. Not even Tom Waller.

Tom Waller... He calls himself a newsman. He'll be finished after all this, and his rag of a paper will be used for a fire starter. Sid smiled and then resumed his tirade.

"Ron! Speed that printing press up! Let her rip!"

Ron shook his head in disbelief. This run was for the record books. He wondered if the old press could hold up through the intense treatment.

"Here's another stack!" handing Sid the hot issue.

"Becky! Get in here! Forget the telephone! Let it ring off the hook! Where's Rick? Get him in here, too!" Sid puffed heavily. He was enjoying the pressure. It was like the old days.

"He's in town covering the follow-ups," Becky said timidly.

"I don't care if he is on the moon... Get him back here! It's about time Rick learned what real work is all about!" He rushed back and forth, stacking, stuffing inserts, and rolling papers. Several stacks, unrolled, lay by the front door for the crowd already swelling downtown.

Sid grabbed another stack and turned to lay it on his desk. *Pain! Ooh, that pain again! It's a, I can't describe it... a nagging pain!* Ignoring it, he pushes on. He knew already what it was, so he worked even harder. The cancer was getting worse, but he kept repeating over and over in his mind, *If I kick out, I'll be buried with that trophy in my hands so Waller can't touch it again!*

<u>10:45 a.m.</u>

Hidden Creek was ablaze. In fact, it was roaring like never before. The message was circulating around town and the county at lightning speed. Phone lines were blinking on the board at *The Daily*, but no one answered. Everyone was trying to find out if the ordeal was a hoax. Broadcasting stations, both radio and television, poured into town loaded with gear in their logoed mobile vans. Street reporters buzzed like flies, badgering patrons to ask their opinion on the Ty Walker message. Most questions revolved around the assumption–"Do you think Walker is a kook?"

Downtown was bursting at the seams with out-of-town visitors eager to satisfy their curiosity about the meeting happening that evening. Business was booming, and cash was flowing in. Cafés, stores, and various merchants were running crazy trying to keep up with demand. Hidden Creek was distinctly a three-ring circus without a ring master.

At the same time, other business venues were taking place. Con men, gamblers, prostitutes, and looters who planned later to rob homes after everyone left carried on their operations, and planned them under the guise of "tourists." Pickpocketing was a major concern. Sheriff McMurphy appointed five deputies from citizens he knew were sound and of good reputation to handle just that problem, but that still wasn't enough. Traffic was horrendous. Parking was a nightmare. And in the middle of all the chaos, Sheriff Mac, now a changed man, had peace. All this was in God's will, and he knew it.

12:37 p.m.

Mayor Hal Haddox, a lifetime politician dressed in his best white suit, stood proudly on the platform used specifically for the Fourth of July festivities. He bellowed out a rousing speech welcoming all visitors to Hidden Creek, decrying state policies, and openly running for Governor. Vendors lined the street selling goods from cotton candy to t-shirts fresh off the press with sayings such as, "Hidden Creek–Not Hidden Anymore," "The Great Walker Roundup," and "Walker or Wacko?" The smell of barbecue flooded the cool air, causing ravenous visitors to divvy up tourist cash. Red, white, and blue balloons, ordered by the city council, lined the streets tied to old city lamps and parking meters. The sound of children squealing in excitement resounded through the heavily occupied roadways. For a Saturday in the middle of

January, it was an absolutely eventful day in the history of Hidden Creek.

1:00 p.m.

Civic organizations rapidly set up 4-H, Parent-Teacher Organization, and Farm Club booths to raise needed funds while the getting was good. Hot apple pie with cinnamon spice, covered with chocolate cream and cherry ooze, was snatched up at lightning speed by the hunger-starved throng. Luke Snider, an antique dealer, moved most of his shop into the open and sold half of his merchandise. Other merchants followed suit after witnessing his success.

A local country and western band, now taking the place of Mayor Haddox on the election stage, blared out the latest from Nashville, while cloggers danced on Main Street in colorful dresses and outfits. The youngsters of the community had a stickball game going at Leslie Field on the corner of Main and Fifth. And on the spur of the moment, Lacy Turner and Greg Matthews tied the knot with wedding vows performed in front of Matthews Bootery by Greg's grandfather, Isaiah Matthews, now a retired ordained elder. The gathering gave a rousing hurrah to the new bride and groom.

Meanwhile, Pastor Stoddard and his wife prayed at the altar of the Community Church. This was not ordinary prayer, but intense agony-type petitions for the entire town, for the visitors, and the congregation. God was speaking to them about what was going on. God was moving. God was preparing.

4:45 p.m.

Hidden Creek residents and visitors began feeling the effect of all the activity and started to wind down. The bustle of the town was settling, and local merchants who perceived the day was nearly done, moved their products back into their stores. Campers and trailers leading away from town lined up at the two locals Rip-N-Jip's for gas and last-minute goodies, which were nearly empty from the hustle and bustle. Residents all over town were seen loading up their vehicles with blankets, chairs, and lanterns. Others took last-minute security measures to protect their homes from looters.

Not everyone was concerned. Those who had decided the invitation was hogwash sat on their front porches watching the melee that was going on, and yelled loud insults at the numerous cars passing by.

Cal Tanner, son of Jake Tanner, who lived on Main Street at the end of town, was mad and nauseated from the whole ordeal. In fact, he had invited some old friends and their families over for an all-night party on his large property. Special invitees were the Gilmores, Driscolls, and Tuckers. In fact, it was open to anyone else who cared to come. It was to relive old times and primarily criticize the foolishness of what was happening in town, as well as the proceedings later at Eagle Point Rock.

6:00 p.m.

Thump! The cue ball plopped into the corner pocket. Melvin Grimes had scratched on the pool game he was involved in with his brother, Lonnie. Both were intoxicated. Lonnie gave a mischievous smile and broke down in laughter at his brother's expense. Melvin didn't appreciate that.

"Ten straight wins! I could beat you left-handed with broken fingers!" bragged Lonnie.

Melvin tapped the top of the table with his stick in frustration.

"Rack 'em, brother! And lay a ten spot beside the rack because I intend to take it from you!"

Lonnie grinned and chuckled, "Easy money. Too easy..." and laughed out loud.

"Bartender!" slurred a drunken Joanne Cassidy. She slapped the top of the bar, yelling, "Where's my drink? What's that Ellie girl doing? Sluffing on the job?"

Bob Casey poured her a double scotch. "Up on the hill she is. Told her she would be fired if she didn't show up today. You see how busy we are!"

Joanne peers across the scene, looking at the unusual crowd. "She went up there with all those nuts, eh?"

"Yep! Seems like most of the town went to hear Walker, except us, who know better. The only hearing that needs to be done is his echoing voice in a jail cell," Bob chuckled.

"Some folks think God told him to go up there," interjected Sam Hardin.

Bob Casey, a known atheist, grew angry and snarled, "Mr. Hardin, how many times have I told you? There is no God! Now get outta' here or shut your yap!"

Sam lifted his shot of whiskey. Every eye in the bar was upon him. Before the glass reached his lips, he stopped and set it down. He reached for his ratty, worn hat and headed for the door.

"And good riddance to you and what you call your make-believe God!" shouted Bob through the snickering and laughter. "Drinks on the house for all right-thinking godless people!" At that, everyone voiced their approval.

Joanne Cassidy slapped the counter and said in a slur, "Yep! We are right-thinkers."

Outside, Sam cranked his old Plymouth station wagon. He stared into the darkness for a moment and finally put the car into gear and made his way to the mountain road. Repeatedly, he whispered, "I believe there is a God. I believe. I believe..."

Chapter 21
Providence

Bulging. Eagle Point was bulging with people—young and old, camera crews, radio, and media teams broadcasting live from the scene. Reporters were as numerous as fleas on a mangy old coonhound. Standing nearby were agents from the county, but for a different reason: to serve a warrant for the arrest of Tyrel Walker. They refrained from taking him for fear of a riot from the crowd, and like the others, a sense of curiosity held their attention. They, too, wanted to see what this was all about.

Laurie Walker pried her way with her two children as far to the front as possible with the help of Deputy North. Even so, he could not get them to the very front because of the mass of people. North had been assigned crowd control (a ridiculous plight).

In the distant background of the crowd, North's patrol car flashed blue and red, creating eerie colors against the hillside that reflected minerals in the soil. Lanterns and flashlights dotted the area like a giant Christmas tree. Deputy North noticed many of his neighbors guiding the Walkers to the front, and many of them hurled insults primarily at Laurie, who said nothing. Deputy North also warned them to keep the peace.

6:58 p.m.

Sheriff McMurphy wheeled his patrol car down Main Street at high speed, lights flashing to scare the daylights out of anyone who considered burglary. He had already picked up two very young thieves who were handcuffed in the rear seat. Mac planned to keep the boys with him because no one was at the jail to tend to them. They rocked back and forth from the rapid turns around town, staring into the night and remained silent.

7:00 p.m.

A hush swept over the assembly as two figures emerged on the grassy bank above the crowd. Cameras snapped to attention, lenses adjusting to capture every second of what was unfolding. It was Moe and Ty. Moe led Ty carefully to the edge, while his head was bowed beneath a hood. Confusion rippled through the audience. Radio reporters murmured play-by-play descriptions from scattered corners of the area. Their voices, however, seemed to fade beneath the weight of anticipation. Then Moe stepped forward, lifting his hand to calm the noises. Every eye was locked on him. The crowd was holding its breath.

"Peoples! Peoples! 'Tention please! Tonight, Mr. Walker will reveal to you what the Lawd's promised many years gone by..."

Wiping tears from his eyes, Moe was full of joy to see that the day had come. Moe backs up and stands at Ty's right side.

Ty reaches up and pulls off the hood.

Laurie screams. The crowd gasps. The first ten rows draw back in awe, searching for breath. Producers and operators yelling and adjusting their light filters in a panicked fashion, trying to focus on the brilliant illumination beaming from Ty Walker's face!

Rick Rider pries open Nettie's fingers from digging into his arm and gazes in wonder at the scene before him. He's mouthing, *"What is this?"* Sid Brumley clutches his chest, feeling discomfort.

As the initial shock wears off, Ty raises his right hand and speaks through the light of his radiant face:

> **"Thus says the Lord, the Lord God of Israel, who
> made Heaven and Earth. I have heard the
> cries of My servants, My faithful who seek Me
> day and night. Their delight is not in what
> they possess, but what they have become
> in Me..."**

Many in the crowd began murmuring about coming all the way up there to hear a sermon. Some began to mock Ty as he continued speaking.

Ty's voice roars louder and clearer:

> **"They who murmured in the desert wandered
> forty years and were finally left to die in the
> barren lands, never to enjoy God's promised
> land and rest!"**

The rowdy people jeered even louder. "Talk about leaving!"

screeched a woman near the front. "You left your wife! Where's that hussy you've been running around with?"

"Hypocrite! That's what he is!" yelled a man.

"Yeah! Hypocrite! Thief!" resounded from numerous places among the mockers.

Deputy North was growing concerned. The groundswell he feared the most had already begun. Hate was rising in pitch, and he was only one man. Even with the help of a few federal officials, they were no match for this mob. Pushing his way back toward his car, the crowd grew nasty, picking up rocks, pelting Ty and Moe with gravel, and screaming insults.

"Adulterer!"
"Wife abuser!"
"Thief!"
"Crook!"
"Jailbird!"

Moe covered Ty's face with his heavy coat and stood directly in front of him, taking the brunt of the beating from the rain of rocks that increased in fury. He winced in pain from the stinging gravel while imagining the pain Jesus must have felt as they crucified him.

Laurie was crying. Begging. Pleading. "No! Lord, please, no!"

A large, gruff farmer told her to shut up. Ben Walker spoke up to him, and the farmer sent the teenager sprawling with a backhand slap. With his lips bleeding, Ben grabs his mother and sister and tries to protect them.

Chaos breaks out, and then... **Boom! Boom!** Standing on the hood of his patrol car, Deputy North had pumped two rounds from his shotgun into the air while the crowd ducked for cover.

"All right! That is enough!" he shouts with all the authority he could muster into his loudspeaker. "We came here tonight to hear

Ty Walker... and that is what we intend to do! If you don't want to give the man a chance, I suggest you leave now!"

Breathing heavily and scared half out of his wits, Will is relieved to see the Feds draw near to him with pistols high in the air to show they meant business. One of them shouts to the crowd, "You heard the man!"

Murmuring stirs among them, as several begin leaving. The large farmer who struck Ben had parting words to the Walker family: "May I never see you people again," as he scooped up some earth from the ground and threw it at them. One of the vocal women near Laurie looked at her and said with disgust, "Christians? Huh?" and spat in her face. Laurie wiped her face without a word. Ty started weeping for the many departures while Moe tried to encourage Ty. Moe is staring directly into Ty's glaring eyes and declares, "Those who have ears will hear."

After a lengthy time, Deputy North declares, "Okay, Ty, you can continue..."

7:15 p.m.

Jesse Tucker, assistant operator at Massey Dam, jerked suddenly from his half-sleeping condition to see the slow blinking yellow light on the main control board. Rushing to the door leading outside, he finds Charles Dunlap, Chief Turbine Supervisor, checking conditions.

Seeing his coworker's semi-panicked face, he asks, "Jesse, what's up?"

"Charles," somewhat out of breath, "we have a problem!"

The yellow light on the control panel has now switched to an ominous flashing red. "Jumping Jehosophat!" cries Charles as he enters and begins throwing switches and checking gauges as fast as he can. He was using all his years of experience to stop what he knew should not be happening. He finally grabs some manuals and quickly fingers for information on procedures for stopping the flashing warning light. Grabbing his binoculars, he rushes out the door. His heart is pounding and his blood pressure is rising! Jesse follows on his heels, pulled by the fear and expression on his boss's face!

"What's going on? I've never seen this before!" shouted Jesse.

"Got to check for water on the seventh sector!" Charles yells above the humming noise of the dam turbine. They raced down the steel staircase, left, then down again, getting faster at each turn. Out of the corner of Charles's eye, he thinks he sees a small trickle of water running down the main face of the dam some thirty yards away. Using his binoculars and the lighting from the main overhead spotlights, he confirms his greatest fear—water! He follows the stream upward, back, and forth, until he comes to a dark and jagged-looking area. With an ashen face, he drops the binoculars as if a man who's given up. His hands trembling.

"Charles! What is it?" yelled Jesse. The anxiety was overwhelming.

"Breach!" screams Charles, he shouts over the noise in terrified fear. "Beginning breach!"

7:25 p.m.

"Years ago," declares Ty, **"your forefathers came to this land, a good land, to make a life for themselves. And so, they did. They poured their heart and soul into everything they put**

their hands to. They honored God, and He blessed them. But not all. Not all honored the Lord. Soon after, the beginnings of wickedness crept into this town he called his own. The wickedness of a strong aroma made him sorry that the man came here. Mixed with that aroma was the cry of blood—the bloodshed of those who fell into evil hands. From the least to the greatest, their blood cries to God from the Earth. Calen McWhorter's murdered blood cries out…"

As Ty declared those words, the McWhorter clan, which descended from Irish immigrants around the turn of the century, began to weep and wail. For many years, they had never learned what had happened to their great-grandfather, who mysteriously disappeared one day in 1929. Others around them gathered closer and consoled them in their grief.

Ty recited name after name with their cause of death: **Josh Murray, Mary Ricards, Eliza Combs, Carey O'Connor, Dalton Oliver, Otis Kimmons, Lila and Moses Wilson**—and a long list of others poured from the lips of Ty Walker upon the stunned listeners. Uncontrolled weeping broke out among the crowd. Entire families fell to their knees in grief over their loved ones. It was like a deep, hidden pain, a dark secret that had been exposed, a history of a sore uncovered. And God was moving upon them in compassion and healing. Rider, Nettie, and Brumley, standing by federal officials, stared dumbfoundedly at the drama.

7:39 p.m.

Charles Dunlap frantically rifles through the emergency manual for procedures involving a condition of breach. He moves his finger left to right, reading at warp speed, realizing every second counted. Thousands of lives were at stake.

"Notify State Water Resource Authorities, County, and Local Officials immediately if a suspected breach occurs. Secure all important files and equipment if possible." Charles resounds the instructions aloud so Jesse can hear.

"Jesse, get the Hidden Creek Sheriff Department on the phone. I'll take care of the State and county! If you can't reach the Sheriff, call Mayor Haddox. Call them at home! Just get somebody! Anybody!"

Jesse punches the numbers, but hits the wrong ones from nervousness. He finally reaches the police department, whose phone rings and rings and rings...

Sheriff McMurphy turned onto Bell Lane and roared down the narrow side road with lights flashing. The two young passengers, in the back—who had already resolved to the fact that Mac was taking them with him no matter where he went for the night—grew weary of being tossed around in the back of the patrol car. Mac whipped onto Main Street once more, lights blaring as he drove erratically. He spots one looter who scurries rapidly into a narrow two-alleyway. Mac stops and peers several minutes, hoping to scare off whoever it was.

At that time, Mac hears the inner whisperings of the Spirit of God. ***"Leave."***

"My Lord and My God!" blurts Mac, surprising the two in the back.

Again, the Spirit speaks to Mac. ***"Leave town now."***

Mac flips a U-turn on Main and floors the pedal of his patrol car as he speeds out of town. He did not let up until he neared the winding curves of the mountain road. He noticed a strange sight through his way up—a parade of cars coming back down to town!

7:45 p.m.

"Mr. Hammond, this is Charles Dunlap, Massey Dam Chief Engineer. We have a major problem. I have detected a breach on the seventh sector, and I need authorization to flood to prevent pressure from creating a much worse situation."

"How serious is the breach?" Water Resource Authority Director Hammond diplomatically says not wanting to be bothered. A very buxom blonde lady, controlled by a lusting spirit which Hammond had no clue was affecting him, had his attention with a million-dollar smile and a figure across the table. She licked her lips, and Hammond nearly dropped his phone.

"Sir, have you lost your senses?" Charles exclaimed in disbelief. "Any breach is critical! If I put off doing a manual and controlled flood any longer, there may not be anything left to save!"

"Now, now. No reason to come unglued. Tell you what, I will call back in say, thirty," glancing at the blonde with a smile, "minutes after you have calmed down. If the situation gets any worse, I will give authorization to flood. Just calm down."

Click. Dial tone.

Charles hangs up. He's stunned and in disbelief. He turns to Jesse, "Any luck with Hidden Creek?"

Jesse shook his head no. "Seems the whole town has vanished!"

Then it dawned on Charles that Jesse was right. This was the night of the Tyrel Walker invitation. *Maybe there was a God looking out on him tonight.*

~

TY STOOD TALL, held up his right hand, and through the outbreak of weeping, he proclaimed:

> **"Today, when you hear His voice, do not harden your hearts. For today is the day of your salvation to you and those afar off. How shall we escape if we neglect such a great salvation? God's desire is that none of you perish this day or, worse yet, perish in the eternal hereafter. It is His providence. His providence to all who listen and hear His voice."**

At this, the few remaining hecklers could be heard above the crying and moaning, but not in the heart of Sid Brumley. Leaving his companions, he drifts closer toward Ty. It was as if he was being magnetized by a message that was working on his heart and mind. Others in the crowd followed suit with the same reaction.

~

7:55 p.m.

NO CALL FROM HAMMOND... Charles nervously paced back and forth by the phone. He would have to do something soon, or it may be too late. He had Jesse posted up on the main lookout to monitor the problem. Charles jumps when Jesse jerks the door open with panic on his face.

"It's getting worse, and the water is coming in greater quantity!" gasped Jesse.

Charles grabs the crucial records and loads them into Jesse's arms. "Get outta here! Now! Throw these into your backseat and head for Eagle Point. I'll be there shortly!"

"But... what are you going to do?"

"I'm trying to give the nitwit Hammond a few more minutes! Now get going!" showing his concern for his friend and coworker. Frantically rushing into the night, Jesse loads the records and speeds off in his pickup toward Eagle Point.

"Come on, Hammond," growing impatient, gritting his teeth, and tapping his fingers on the hardwood desk. His eyes never left the phone.

Then he heard it. An awful grinding, grating sound that sent terror to his bones. The moment of finality had reached the point of no return. Charles paused at the door, his hand hovering over the emergency siren handle. Thirty-one years...and he never thought he would do this. He grips the handle and yanks it hard to the right. The siren screeches into the evening air. He doesn't look back. The phone rings on the desk, unanswered. *Let it ring*, he thinks. *No one left to answer it now.*

THE CROWD JUMPED in response to the siren, and murmuring broke out all over the area about what it might mean. Intermixed with the siren, a low rumbling came from the depths of the earth. Some screamed, thinking it was an earthquake. Others, a bomb.

Speculation grew louder and louder in the multitude. Ty and Moe stood still, heads bowed, letting God do His will.

Jesse pulled into Eagle Point, lights flashing, blowing his horn repeatedly. He slid to a halt, just missing a media van in the gravel and the dirt. Jumping out, he screams, "Massey Dam! It is breaking up!"

The crowd was numb. Stunned. In a matter of moments, all they owned, worked for, had, and knew would soon be destroyed, and there was nothing on earth to stop the onslaught of power now being unleashed on their property.

The rumbling grew louder as trees ripped from the landscape, flowing like missiles in the surge of water. More than a million cubic feet roared through the valley, taking everything in its path. The large oak, symbolically, on which Lila and Moses were hung, came down with a snap.

Inside Casey's bar, the Tucker brothers stopped their game and stood with the others, peering outside and feeling the rumblings of the ground.

Screams! Then panic! The next second, they were no more as the water and its weapons flattened and washed everything in sight downstream. The sound of shearing metal, wood, and rushing water echoed throughout the region. Hidden Creek was no more... every structure, home, business, bank, school, and church—gone.

Back at Eagle Point, most were crying. All their possessions were destroyed except their very own lives. Many began to realize the importance of that fact.

Sid, fifteen feet from Ty and Moe, cried aloud, "You saved our lives! My life!" He was wailing and falling to his knees. All who heard Sid began saying the same thing, and the words spread like wildfire through the crowd.

Ty looked at the group and said in a bold voice:

"God has granted you His providence this day. Everything you possessed is now gone, except your own soul. When you examine life, you will discover that it is truly all you have. It is now up to you to give what you really own, that is, yourself to God and believe in the Lord Jesus Christ."

Sid Brumley jumped up and came forward, tears streaming down his face and bellowing, "May God forgive me!"

"He will, Sid," Ty says bluntly. He walks over and places his hand on Sid's chest. "And God also heals." Sid takes a deep breath... his first good deep breath in years! The cancer was gone, and he knew it! Rejoicing and jumping around, he repeatedly shouts, "I believe! It's gone! My cancer is gone!" Sid exclaims the news of his miraculous healing to the crowd.

Doc Waters, the physician of Hidden Creek who had been treating Sid, marveled. So much so, he pushed and shoved his way to the front. "Do you think the Lord can forgive an old goat like me? I've used these hands and this mind for years. I have seen people recover who couldn't have without some divine help, and yet, my intellect stood in the way. I have denied that God is real for all my career." Repeating his original question, he fell to his knees with his hands to his face.

"Yes, without a doubt, Doc," replied Ty with a smile. In an instant, Doc Waters joined the kingdom! One by one, they came, entire families, each finding God and His forgiveness. Confessions were piping up all over the camp. The presence of the Holy Spirit was strong and moving. News crews dropped their cameras and equipment to the ground, leaving their vans and setups behind. They, too, found mercy and grace. Weeping broke out once more, this time, however, tears of joy and gladness by the power of the Holy Spirit.

Laurie Walker and family were also weeping. Ty walked through the mass of bodies and extended his arms to his family. Laurie's lips trembled and mouthed the words, "I love you." She flung her arms around his neck, and makeup and tears were running down her face. Ben hugged his father's side while Audrey clung to one of his legs. They were laughing and crying together.

Others were not so happy. Nettie, Rick, and a couple of townsfolk were disgusted with the scene before them. Their focus was on deciding where to go and what they were going to do.

"Rick, let's go to Nashville! We can find work and be together forever!" she squealed, seeing an opportunity to be with him. Rick stared at her, revealing his inner self.

"I wouldn't go across the road with you! It is about time you come to grips with the fact that I used you to get what I wanted, and now I have my story... so you can beat it!"

Nettie blinked, holding back tears. "What?"

Angry as a demon, Rick Rider snorted, "You heard me! Get lost!" Nettie exploded in tears as she ran away.

Soon, a song rose above the camp, singing from hearts of joy and praise. The melodious sound went on into the night about the wonders and grace of the Lord. They were in no hurry to go. They had no place to go...

Chapter 22
Beginnings

Late spring flowers dotted the newly paved road, displaying the rebuilding of the town of Hidden Creek. Completely destroyed, construction crews with enormous bulldozers plowed and piled the giant mass of debris to the east of the city. Surveyors worked long, tireless hours determining property boundaries by examining the corner foundations that could be found. Most of the recognizable scenery had been washed downstream or buried under a layer of dirt, mud, and silt.

Federal officers stood watch over the bank vault, now relocated sixty yards from its original site, until a new building could be erected to ensure its security. Emergency medical funds, supplies, food, and water poured in from all over the state to help the community recover.

Most people lived in tents sent from the National Guard in Sipley, cooked over open fires, and enjoyed the fresh air. Townsfolk felt blessed that the remainder of the winter and early spring season remained mild with infrequent snowfall, and they kept a spirit of thankfulness for how God saved them... Saved them indeed.

An overwhelming majority had a heartwarming, soul-changing experience during the previous four months. Professions of faith were heard frequently three nights a week when the town would come together in the *"Gathering of the Tents"* to sing and hear three local preachers speak. Baptisms provided a celebratory event as hundreds would gather and applaud the new believers.

Homes and business buildings were being erected at a record pace. Entire families converged in helping one another with framing, sheet-rocking, and roofing. Plumbers and electricians from Sipley and surrounding cities congregated and worked tirelessly, happy to meet the needs.

Hidden Creek High School was now half completed, which served as a symbol that the town was coming back. The ancient oaks, once decorating the grounds, now gone, were replaced by small trees lining the school grounds. The elementary school was nearly complete and was already holding classes for grades one through nine from 7:00 a.m. to 12 noon and grades ten through twelve from 1:00 p.m. to 6:00 p.m. Funds supplied by the state and federal government were providing teachers' pay, books, and all the students' needs. Chaotic, yes, in rebuilding, but this devastated community united in the same way the Holy Bible tells us to:

"Love your neighbor as yourself."

— MARK 12:31

THE DAILY WAS ALREADY BACK in business. A small building was erected, and the printer and all equipment were donated by the *Nashville Times*. Weekly reports supplied news to locals concerning the goings-on of the town and any volunteer projects. Sid Brumley, healed from cancer, had dramatically changed the outlook of the paper. No more destructive character assassinations. No more rumors. No more lies. In fact, he added a section in the paper for professions of faith in Christ and testimonies. Sid focused on the good aspects of the news, for it had been negative far too long.

Rick Rider was not a happy camper. Juicy news he considered important was turned down immediately by Sid. At every turn, he was frustrated. Rick even missed Nettie, who had left for Nashville for good. He had heard the rumors that Nettie had met a nice man who had led her to Jesus Christ, and now she was going to church and planning her marriage. The very thought was enough to make him gag. Still, he had one last card to play—Tom Waller. And since the *Sipley Sun* covered all the aftermath of the Massey Dam disaster, Rick figured *The Sun* had no competition for the story of the year.

Making his way to Sid's office, Rick hands him another story of character assault, a story concerning the alcohol problem of a politician in a nearby town.

"Sid, look at this. It might be just the story to get us going again," he says with an evil smirk and intent.

Sid skims the piece, tosses it aside, and says nothing.

"Well?" Rick presses.

"Well, what, Rick? You know I'll not cover that trash. He probably has enough troubles without us dragging him into print. It's nothing but trash."

"Trash! This is a great story! Public interest!" Rick responds, yelling with force.

"Whose interest? Yours perhaps?" Sid replies, adjusting his glasses.

"I didn't know as a reporter I'd be hindered by all this compassion stuff. If I'd known this long ago, I would not have worked for this small-time outfit!" Rick snarls, proceeding to pull out his trump card.

"Tom Waller at the *Sipley Sun* will get the county story of the year trophy… no doubt this time with your reluctance to print any story!" seethes Rick.

Sid clears his throat, slowly standing.

Bingo, thought Rick. *I've got him now.*

Very calmly, Sid speaks. "Rick, you are right on two accounts. One, *The Sun* will get story of the year, and two, you no longer work here." Sid sits down peacefully.

Rick was stunned. "What? You're firing me? Rick Rider?"

"Just letting you go is a better term. I need someone with a better outlook and an optimistic attitude, and you no longer, or never have, fit that mold. See Becky and pick up your pay. Oh, and one more thing… Rick, you will never find the real story until you find Jesus Christ. Search for Him as you search for dirt, and you will find Him. I'll be praying for you."

Speechless, Rick bumps into a chair and stumbles out.

Moments later, Sid dials a number. It was Tom Waller at *The Sun.*

"Tom. Sid here. Just called to say that your paper did such a great job on the collapse of Massey Dam and Hidden Creek. You showed real insight into what we all suffered. And oh yeah… I buried the hatchet against you. Just wanted to say I am sorry for all the years I strived to be better than you."

Tom Waller smiles on the other end. "Accepted with gladness in my heart, Sid. When you get caught up with all your rebuilding, how about you and I go fishing at Mirror Lake like we used to?"

"You're on!" Sid replies. He leans back in his chair and clasps his hands behind his head. *What a great day for the good news.*

In the next room, Ron awkwardly enters Becky's makeshift office. Papers and files lay scattered everywhere, still in search of a proper place to be stacked. Her new telephone system was having problems, with technicians constantly coming in and out. She was having a tough time adjusting to the little room and to the new system. She rubs her eyes wearily, clearly showing the toll it was taking on her.

"Becky? How are you doing?"

"Not very well right now, Ron, but like I always say, 'Life is great,' and I'm sure it will be better tomorrow," she replies, flashing a small, forced smile.

"I... I wanted to tell you... ehh... ask you something," Ron said shyly.

"Yeah?" her interest piquing.

Ron gathers all his courage. "During and after the flood, one thought kept coming to me over and over."

"What was that, Ron?"

Taking a deep breath, he replies, "What would my life have missed if I had never asked you for a date. I care very much for you, and I'd be honored if you would go out with me Friday night."

Oh! It's finally happening! Internally, Becky squeals from her excitement. Then, gathering her inner composure, she replies with a soft smile, "I'd love to." The days of frustration were now only a faint memory.

TY WALKER WIPES the sweat from his forehead due to the warmer days of summer. He, Moe, and several volunteers were diligently working on the school grounds alongside crews building a new parking lot at the high school.

The hearty shrubs were filling in the bare sections along the front entrance. It gladdened his heart to see so many of the townspeople come out to help—people who would have never stepped up before. All of them felt a greater purpose: to get Hidden Creek back into operation as soon as possible.

Ty ceases his work when he notices a new Buick pulling up. Maggie Stewart steps out with a beaming smile. A handsome, distinguished man joins her as they walk together toward Ty.

"Maggie!" Ty exclaims in a glad voice.

"Oh, Ty!" She let go of her escort's hand and instantly threw her arms around Ty's neck. "It's so good to see you!" Looking back, she introduces her companion.

"Ty, this is Marshall, my ex... eh... my husband." She smiled sheepishly from the embarrassment of using the prefix *ex*. "We were remarried five days ago!"

"Marshall, this is Tyrel Walker, my friend and—still—boss, I hope."

"The job belongs to you. I wouldn't have it any other way," Ty replies.

"I want to thank you, Ty, for all you have done for me. Without your help and support, well, I wouldn't have made it. Besides, I have my husband back. There is no way I can repay you for your kindness."

Ty and Marshall shake hands, exchanging pleasantries and talking about the town, the rebuilding, and the likes. Marshall, a real estate agent with a successful business in Washington, D.C., expressed his fatigue with the city's hassles and how he was looking forward to moving to the area for a new start in the country.

Maggie abruptly jumps into the conversation. "I heard you were a jailbird for a week."

Smiling, Ty responds. "They held me after the disaster for five days, that's all. Dill County officials apologized for the trouble caused by an accounting error that resulted in missing funds. It is now in the past, and part of God's plan. I had the privilege to witness to the Chief of Police, Sheriff Watkins, about Jesus Christ, and he accepted Christ in the cell with me."

Maggie shook her head in amazement.

A tooting horn interrupts the reunion. Laurie Walker and family pull to a stop in the unpaved section of the driveway. Out jump Ben and Audrey as if they had been caged up. Laurie was busily working with the car seat.

"Miss Maggie!" shouts Audrey in happiness. The youngster leaps into the waiting arms of Maggie. "We sure missed you, Miss Maggie!"

"I have missed all of you, too!" And then Maggie sees what Laurie had been busy with—a baby.

"The baby! Oh my!" She gazes into the face of the precious infant and reaches out to hold him.

"A boy!"

"Yes," beams Ty.

"What's his name?"

"Orren Hastings Walker."

"Well, that's a fine name!" Maggie replies as she cuddles and coos over the baby as if she were the mother. "When was he born?"

"January 30; eight days after the flood."

"Oh, Ty, I'm so happy for you and Laurie!"

Ty was about to respond when Laurie naggingly poked him in the side. Her focus was on the road leading to the school. In disbelief, they all begin to stare at the man approaching on a slow-walking horse.

"Ty, is that who I think it is?" Maggie asks

"It sure is," he answers at the same time as Moe.

It was Oliver Wendell Huber! Oliver had not been in the city limits of Hidden Creek in close to fifty years. Everyone stopped what they were doing, dropping shovels and rakes, gawking at the old man on the dapple-gray mare. Oliver dismounted clumsily and tied his horse to a tree, allowing it to graze on the little grass that existed. Limping toward all of them, he reveals a happy, toothless smile.

"Hi-dy folks! Moe…" He tips his hat.

Everyone was speechless. No one moved. A great deal of time passes before Ty finally pierces the silence.

"Good to see you, Oliver!" Ty reaches out to shake his weathered hand. "We're surprised to see you in town." With the knowledge of the journal, he understood Oliver's history and why he avoided Hidden Creek for the longest time.

"Bout time, I reckon to see me ol' mug mingling with the folks. I used to, you know." He takes off his hat and shakes his bald head. "Things sure'n have changed 'round here."

"We are getting the town back together, slowly but surely, Oliver. How are you doing?"

"Ah… you know… the dam is in the process of construction, and it will be quite a while for fishing to start again, but I have me animals to care for and provide me some grub." As Maggie walked by with the baby in her arms, Huber pipes up, "What pray tell 'tis this?" chuckles Huber. His bare gums shine as he looks at baby Orren.

"Your'n, ma'am?"

"No, not mine, Mr. Huber. He belongs to the Walker family."

"I's figured as much," he laughed. "Last time I saw the miss, I could tell right off she was spectin'."

"His name is Orren. Orren Hastings Walker," Ty interjects, seeking a response from Oliver, which he got.

"As in Orren Hastings, the ol' Hermit Hastings?

"One and the same."

"I ain't heard or spoken that name in more than fifty to sixty years! He was an arguing ol' cus, but he was me friend."

"He spoke highly of you also. He wrote about your good deeds, your kindness to the downtrodden, like Moe Wilson. He also spoke about your preaching. In fact, there's a lot about you I never knew."

When Ty mentioned the preaching, everyone gasped in surprise at Oliver.

The old man shuffles his feet around in the dirt, and his hands begin to pull at the pockets of his bib overalls. He was embarrassed to have his life exposed in front of the others, which made him very uncomfortable.

"Twas a long time ago," he says in a low voice. "I let a lot of things go back yonder. A lot of things let go of me."

"There's one thing that hasn't let you go, Oliver," Ty says gently, realizing the opportunity to speak to this dear man. He places his hand on Oliver's back and leads him down the dirt drive away from the others.

"You ever heard the words of a song that goes 'O love that won't let me go'?"

Oliver nods, "Yep, sure'n have."

While the others watched, the two men walked away from the group side by side. Ty's left hand was expressing an important detail while Oliver limped and nodded his head approvingly, yanking at his sagging overalls that told the story of better years.

MAY WE ALL HEAR THAT STORY
AND HAVE IT IN OUR HEARTS!

About the Author

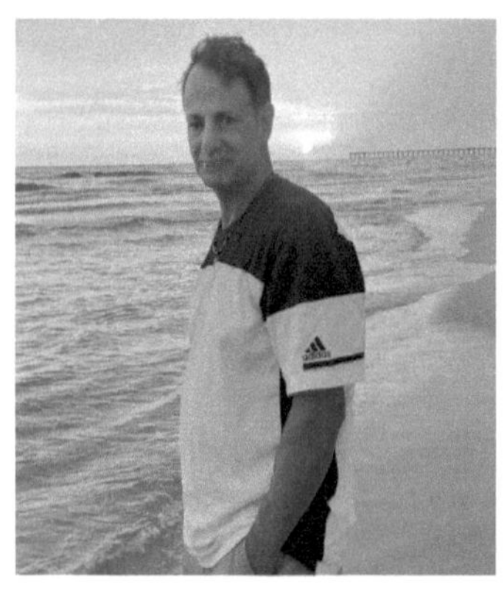 **Eddie Harden** is a Southern-born storyteller with a heart grounded in faith and a life shaped by service. A retired minister with over 40 years in the Church of the Nazarene, Eddie has dedicated decades to guiding others as an Assistant Pastor, Senior Pastor, and youth teacher. But long before the pulpit, Eddie wore the uniform of the U.S. Air Force. This was a stark difference from when he was just a kid growing up in Adamsville, Alabama, running wild through small-town streets with a head full of big dreams.

That "big dream" changed its scope when he accepted Christ in 1983 at the age of 25, led by the faithful prayers of a Birmingham city bus driver who called his name at every red light for over a year. It was a relief to everyone who had experienced his non-Christian life. Four months after his life transformation, Eddie preached his first sermon and never looked back. Today, his writing reflects that same passion with simple, heartfelt stories that speak to the everyday believer, pointing always to the faithfulness of God.

Now, he contentedly lives in Milton, Florida, with his wife, Rhonda, of nearly 47 years, who was also his childhood neighbor. Eddie fills his days with guitar playing, coin collecting, fishing, and tracking down *The Andy Griffith Show* autographs.

Eddie is a firm believer that even in life's hardest chapters, God never fails to fulfill His promises. Through Christian fiction rooted in hope and grit, Eddie Harden invites readers to remember:

With Jesus, we have everything.
Without Him, we have nothing.

You can help keep the story going by following Eddie Harden's socials:

Thank You For Your Support!

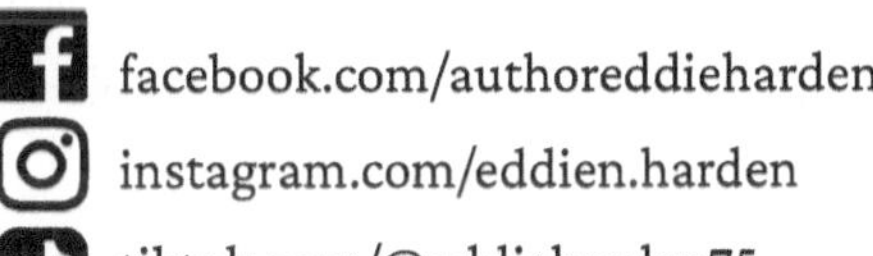

About the Publisher

PipStones Publishing

"Weavers of Tales and Tellers of Truth"

MISSION STATEMENT:

Our mission is to publish unique and refreshing works of various authors and genres; to present and highlight literary endeavors in an ever-changing marketplace.

SERVICES:

Editing, Formatting, Illustrating, Publishing, Distributing, Local & Social Marketing, Author Coaching

NOTE TO AN AUTHOR:

Our goal is to walk with you through every step of your publishing journey.